CREW ROSTER

Ian Randal Strock

Robert E. Waters

Danielle Ackley-McPhail

John L. French

Jody Lynn Nye

Christopher M. Hiles

Peter Prellwitz

Judi Fleming

Jeff Young

Nancy Jane Moore

Patrick Thomas

Robert Greenberger

James Chambers

Mike McPhail

**"Earth is the cradle of humanity,
but one cannot remain in the cradle forever."
Konstantin E. Tsiolkovsky**

IF WE HAD KNOWN

Edited by Mike McPhail

eBooks
Pennsville, NJ

PUBLISHED BY
eSpec Books LLC
Danielle McPhail, Publisher
PO Box 242,
Pennsville, New Jersey 08070
www.especbooks.com

ISBN: 978-1-942990-29-1
ISBN (ebook): 978-1-942990-30-7

Design: Mike and Danielle McPhail
Cover Art: © Igor Zh.
Copyeditors: Greg Schauer
             Danielle McPhail, www.sidhenadaire.com

Dedicated to the memory of

Dr. Jeffrey Scott Nye
1959-2017

Neuroscientist, physician, son,
brother, husband, father, and reader of science fiction.

CONTENTS

THE NECESSARY ENEMY

Ian Randal Strock

YANG AND YIN, LIGHT AND DARK, GOOD AND EVIL. THE PHILOSOPHERS have known all along. But seeing the applicability of philosophy to real life has never been humanity's strong suit.

If we had realized that it takes a villain to make a hero. If we had realized that we needed an enemy in order to be the victor. If we had realized a ruling party needs a loyal opposition....

"Make America Great Again" started off as a campaign slogan, and became a political rallying cry. But as with most political slogans, it was only half-right. Where the slogan failed was in ignoring the fact that, in order to be great, America had to be compared to something else, had to have an equally great enemy to contend against.

America's rise to greatness began with the Civil War. In those years of horror and death, the Northern states finally came together as a coherent whole, truly a united nation. After the war, it took a long time to integrate the Southern states into that whole.

When Theodore Roosevelt launched the Great White Fleet, he was announcing America's intention to take a major role on the world stage, and by the time of World War I, the USA was on its way to greatness. From the American point of view, the war was brief, giving Americans the impetus to build up to a war footing without the drain of actually fighting a terribly long war. And at war's end, the USA grabbed center stage as a powerful player. Even if the nation rejected Woodrow Wilson's League of Nations, his actions in Paris served notice that the United States was a major player. And then World War II truly brought America to the top of the heap.

But it wasn't simply domestic will that made America a superpower, it wasn't merely the creation of the atomic bomb. It was the fact that we faced enemies of equal stature. During that war, it was Nazi Germany and the Empire of Japan, both of whom were sent to ignominious defeat.

At the end of the war, the leaders of the free world foresaw the rise of the Soviet Union, and promulgated the Bretton Woods agreement to guarantee the peace of the free world. Maintaining that agreement, guaranteeing free passage of the seas, made the USA a superpower.

And the rise of the Soviet Union gave the United States a true adversary, an equal but opposite superpower against whom to contend. Thus, the USSR, more than anything else, is what made America great.

It was because of the USSR that the USA came together to put a man on the Moon. In 1962, John Kennedy spoke at Rice University, and while everyone remembers him saying "we will put a man on the Moon and safely return him to Earth during this decade," it was the reasons leading up to that statement that truly kicked the American space program in the ass. In the prefatory paragraphs of his speech, he said "for the eyes of the world now look into space, to the moon and to the planets beyond, and we have vowed that we shall not see it governed by a hostile flag of conquest, but by a banner of freedom and peace.... Whether it will become a force for good or ill depends on man, and only if the United States occupies a position of pre-eminence can we help decide whether this new ocean will be a sea of peace or a new terrifying theater of war.... Within these last 19 months at least 45 satellites have circled the earth. Some 40 of them were 'made in the United States of America' and they were far more sophisticated and supplied far more knowledge to the people of the world than those of the Soviet Union.... To be sure, we are behind, and will be behind for some time in manned flight. But we do not intend to stay behind, and in this decade, we shall make up and move ahead." It wasn't that the moon was a great place to go; it was that we had to beat the commies to get there. An adversary pushing, not a goal pulling.

And after we won the space race, it was because of the USSR that the USA built the largest, most powerful navy the world had ever known. It was because of the USSR that the USA strove to excel in the sciences, in economics, in pretty much every field of endeavor.

Unfortunately, we slipped up. We didn't think deeply enough about the conflict. We lost sight of our need for the Soviet Union's existence, and started thinking of them as an enemy to actually be defeated. Thus, Ronald Reagan's SDI program—perhaps accidentally—did force the USSR to spend itself into bankruptcy. It wasn't long after that the USSR fell apart, leaving the USA as the world's only superpower. And in the glory of that triumph, we didn't realize it heralded our own coming slide. But George Orwell had pegged that one, with the never-ending war in *1984*.

Without a proper enemy, maintaining our stature as a superpower became a nearly futile exercise. That status began to invite attacks, not by another superpower, but by gnats, mosquitos, tiny groups of feral dogs bent on taking down the biggest kid on the block. Not unlike an elephant, which is able to stomp a lion, but can be taken down by a pack of jackals, the United States was open to attack by tiny groups of religious zealots.

That's why, though we did (unfortunately) win the Cold War, we could never win the "War on Drugs," the "War on Poverty," the "wars" of terrorism, nor defeat any of the other invented, too-small enemies. We could never invent an enemy great enough. Consider *TNG*'s episode, "Elementary, Dear Data": a villain has to be able to win to make the fight worth fighting.

So we find ourselves in need of an enemy. A great enemy. One worthy of our stature.

And we can look beyond our own greatness. As we gathered a coalition of allies to win World War II (and tried to build coalitions for the later, tinier wars), we can once again gather a coalition of nations — if we can present them with a truly great, truly awesome enemy, one that requires our combined efforts.

We need an alien invasion. We don't want Star Trek's Vulcans, lending a helping hand. The self-loathing of *Avatar* would do more to keep us at home. Even the mindless planet-killers of *Armageddon* or *Deep Impact* probably wouldn't serve to elicit our best efforts. What we truly need is *Independence Day*. We need a massive alien invasion that threatens to destroy all life on Earth. That... that would be an enemy awesome enough and mighty enough to make us once again great.

But you know, there's just never an alien invasion around when you need one.

That's why I called you, individually and specifically, here in secrecy within the relative anonymity of the International Space Development Conference. Within this room, I believe, are the minds that can convince the world of a coming alien threat. You were specifically chosen for your backgrounds. Among you we have scientists, engineers, fictioneers... people representing all the fields of human endeavor necessary to convince the public that we face an existential threat, and that we can overcome that threat.

I'll say it before you can: as scientists, we're dedicated to the search for truth. Are we abrogating that public trust if we lie an alien invasion into existence? Yes, in the short term, we probably are. But in the longer term? I think we've all said, at one time or another, that the greatest threat to humanity's survival is not leaving the surface of the planet. So if perpetrating the lie that an alien invasion is coming can be the driving force to get us to expand into space, do you think we could live with ourselves?

What do you say? Shall we get down to the business of lying to humanity?

That recording was made surreptitiously by my great-grandfather. And every day after that conference ended, he devoted himself to helping humanity prepare for the alien threat. For three generations, our family has worked in the great endeavor. But I still believe it was that gathering, that discussion, that was the sole driving force that got humanity off the surface of Earth in a meaningful way, that drove us to develop the orbitals, and Moonbase Artemis, and the *Traveler*. And now, as you're getting ready to join the first wave of humanity to voyage beyond the confines of the Solar System, it's time to pass the burden of knowledge on to you. Only you can decide when or if your fellow travelers will be ready to learn that their voyage is predicated on a myth. That there really is no imminent alien invasion. I leave it to you to decide when they will have reached the stage of saying "If we had known, we would have gone anyway."

THE STEADY DRONE OF SILENCE

Danielle Ackley-McPhail

EXCUSE ME? LIEUTENANT KOLBY…EXCUSE ME!" CHRISTOPHER JAMES SPOKE softly into the headset attached to the helmet the lieutenant had jammed onto his head before they'd left the transport. "I need to know what's gone wrong…"

Just ahead, Kolby snapped around to look over his shoulder, his features hard-set and his gaze unyielding. His posture projected urgency.

Christopher fell silent as he felt his eyes widen and the rest of him go cold. *This must be how a rabbit feels caught in a hawk's sights*, he thought as he swallowed hard and fought the urge to duck his head. Kolby looked away and continued his hurried, but methodical progress through the brush, his eyes continually scanning in all directions, even straight up into the sky.

A shiver ran over Christopher. *Why would the lieutenant look up?*

Clutching the straps of the rucksack holding his tablet computer, he did his best to move as quickly and quietly as the soldiers escorting him. Fat chance of that, though. He was a civilian contractor. An engineer. A tech head specializing in unmanned aerial vehicles, or UAVs. Two weeks ago he'd been pulled from his current research project with no explanation. Now he found himself on the butt end of Demeter traipsing through the wilds, destination unknown. He didn't have to ask to know the soldiers escorting him weren't any happier about it than he was.

Maybe he should have been paying more attention to where he was walking, instead of worrying over where he was going. Abruptly, his forward motion switched to downward as a root or something snagged his foot, tripping him. Christopher started to cry out only to find himself gripped by what felt like two steel bands, one across his mouth, the other around his upper arm. He had the vague impression the rest of the soldiers around him had dropped low to the ground and gone still. Christopher himself couldn't help but tremble as he came eye to up-close eye with Lieutenant Kolby.

"Do you *want* to die?" The words were so low and emphatic Christopher questioned if he'd actually heard them, either way the message was clear in Kolby's gaze.

Christopher shook his head.

Kolby looked over at the soldier to their left. Samson, if Christopher remembered correctly. Hanging from the man's neck was an electronic device. Some kind of tracker-slash-monitor. All Christopher knew was the little green light on the top of the housing meant they were good. If the red one went on, they were screwed. The man nodded and Kolby nodded back. Only then did he release his grip on Christopher. One hand dropped to the rifle hanging from the strap slung across Kolby's chest, the other rose slowly into the air in an obscure gesture Christopher had to guess meant 'proceed', because—as if they were guided by one brain—the six soldiers rose from where they crouched and continued through the brush with barely a sound.

Christopher couldn't move.

The soldier behind him gave him a controlled shove. Not enough to make him fall, but enough to break the grip of the fear anchoring Christopher in place. He was terrified of messing up again. He was terrified of whatever was out there that had Kolby treading so lightly. He was terrified of never making it home.

Christopher had no place being on this mission.

Apparently the military felt otherwise. Or at least someone up the chain of command did.

Christopher just wished he knew what they were thinking because the only thing worse than being out here was having no clue why.

Just before sunset, they stopped to set up camp beneath a stand of saplings. Of course, on Demeter 'sapling' meant the boles were a mere eighteen inches in diameter and the lowest branches fifteen feet over head. Christopher stood just beneath the trees at twilight numbly wondering how he could barely feel his feet, yet at the same time have them burn like fire.

Around him the soldiers raised a light-framed canopy, large enough for all of them to crowd beneath. He watched as they lowered the sides. The fabric was familiar. It woke the echo of a memory in his fogged brain. He reached out to rub a fold between his fingers. Again, familiar, and now he knew why. A plasticized version of the nylon fiber had been used to form the body of a long-flying surveillance drone he'd served as project lead on. It had been just the edge they'd needed to successfully conclude the assignment. Not only was the material ultralight, but micro-circuitry woven among the threads was programmable for several key functions, from camouflaging to shielding to alternate energy absorption. When paired with the focused inboard lasers as an ignition source, latent energy could be converted into accessible power that could then be absorbed by the drone's thermal converter. Their goal had been to create a self-sustaining, self-repairing drone that could remain airborne for a year or more at a consistent altitude.

His team had succeeded.

He was very proud of that project; regretted having had to pass it on to Captain Linda Pierce, and the military's practical testing group. Professional rivalry aside, he more than liked Linda, though nothing much had come of it so far. Kind of hard when the military kept sending her off to remote locations to test his prototypes. Still, he always managed something to ensure she didn't forget about him. This time it had been a gaudy, glittery pin that proudly proclaimed *"I'm #2!"* He'd slipped it in with the transfer papers.

He couldn't wait to see what prank she pulled to get even. Who knew when that would be, though. Practical testing could take months. He hoped she was treating his baby with care. Just before the hand-off, a fire at the research facility had destroyed his final notes for the project before he was able to back them up. He would have to reverse engineer the final stages from the prototype before the drones could go into production.

A familiar grip settled on Christopher's shoulder, yanking him around and away from his thoughts. "Perhaps I wasn't as clear as I believed I was, Mr. James, when this all started. When we had our talk about how to stay alive."

Exhausted and frustrated and more than a little annoyed, Christopher had less control of his tongue than usual. As in none. "Quite clear, Lieutenant Kolby, just not nearly complete enough."

Even as the words left his mouth, Christopher flinched. Kolby's jaw couldn't have jutted harder if it had been carved from granite. Still gripping Christopher's shoulder, he hauled him across to the edge of the canopy, as far as they could get from the other men.

"Excuse me?" Kolby's tone was low and even and completely at odds with his body language.

Sighing, Christopher dropped his gaze, before forcing it up again. It was in his nature to avoid conflict, but this wasn't the lab, and this wasn't going away. If he was already going to catch heat, he might as well speak his piece.

"Lieutenant, I'm not a soldier. I haven't had a soldier's training. I don't know how to move like you need me to. I don't have combat instincts. I haven't been trained to navigate terrain. I don't *know* what I need to watch for, or what I need to avoid."

He could tell by Kolby's furrowing brow that what he was trying to say wasn't getting through.

"Lieutenant Kolby, I'm a civilian, as much as we all need me to act like a soldier I'm never going to be good enough, especially compared to your men. I just don't have the skills." He raised his hands in the classic gesture of 'this is what you get'. "I'm an engineer. I'm assuming that's why I'm on this mission, why else would you go to the trouble… the *risk*…to haul me out here? But I don't have the data I need. I don't know what problem to bend my mind to. I need time to pull a solution out of my ass. If I'm going to be of any use to you, I have to know what's going on before it's in my face."

For a moment, Christopher thought he might have connected, then Kolby's military protocol clearly kicked in.

"Civilian or not, Mr. James, when you are in that uniform, on this mission…you are under my command!" Kolby barked out low and hard, his face bright red and his features twisted in anger. "I will tell you what you need to know, *when* you are authorize to know it. Until then, you bend that pointed little head of yours toward following orders before what's in your *face* is a shit storm!"

Acid bubbled in Christopher's gut as the lieutenant stalked away as far as the tent allowed. He stood there, pale and trembling in the wake of the conflict, forcing himself to remain standing straight. A taut silence hung in the air as the other soldiers went about their duties, clearly aware of the confrontation, but in no way reacting.

Without a word, Christopher moved to his belongings and spread out his bedroll. Before he could lay down, Kolby tossed a ration pack at him. It hit Christopher's chest hard enough it stung. His arms reflexively closed around it.

"Eat, *now*. We're not carrying your ass tomorrow."

Christopher's jaw clenched and his gut spasmed, but he followed orders.

They woke and broke camp before the sunrise did more than flirt with the horizon. Kolby ignored him — thank God — but the soldier from the day before, a dark-skinned man with RANDALL on his name tape and sergeant's stripes on his sleeve, pulled Christopher off to the side before they started the day's march.

"Think of it like a circuit board," Randall said, his gaze darting toward the lieutenant, like he was watching for one of his signals.

Christopher frowned. "What?"

"Moving through the terrain...it's tricky, you have to be careful to avoid notice...like when you're working on a circuit board. You need to know right where to move, and when to move, or you break or fry the circuits. Same with what we're doing here. Be alert, look for what's in your way...twigs beneath your feet, thorns on the bushes, those're the things that'll make you break your connection...so don't. Slow and steady does it, be alert, be focused, move carefully...like you're working on a circuit board." He grinned, and Christopher had to grin back, not exactly feeling good about what lay ahead, but feeling better because Randall's advice made sense and even if it hadn't, the soldier...the *man*...was trying to help him out, like he had yesterday, when Christopher couldn't move.

"Now, pay attention," Randall went on. He moved his hands in a series of gestures, explaining what they stood for as he made each one. "Those are the ones Butter Bar is most likely to use." — it took Christopher a moment to realize Randall was referring to Kolby — "Anything else, you just drop down and stay still if you don't know what the signal means. That'll be safest."

Suddenly, Randall's expression changed, like he was listening to someone Christopher couldn't hear, and there was a faint twitch along his jaw. "Yessir," he muttered, then turned back to Christopher. "Don't worry, man, I'll be watchin' your back."

"Thank you," Christopher said with a nod. As the soldier started to move off, Christopher called to him, keeping his voice low. "Randall… please…what are we doing out here?"

For a moment it looked like the soldier would remain silent, but he darted a defiant look toward his lieutenant's back and then met Christopher's eye. When he spoke, his lips barely moved, "Command has lost contact with the practical testing group working on your UAV; they think the team's gone rogue and are using the drone to secure their position. We need you to crack the controls so we can take it back."

Christopher's chest tightened and his gut dropped as he thought of Linda. He couldn't say a word, couldn't catch a breath. He struggled a moment, then got himself under control. "You can't be serious!"

Across the headset came a burst of static, then Kolby's voice hissed, "Move your asses, NOW!"

Randall gave Christopher an understanding look and clapped his shoulder, then turned to fall into position. Christopher followed, taking his place behind Kolby without a word, his mind struggling with what he'd just been told.

As they made their way across the landscape, moving in at least an approximation of the soldiers' motions became easier as Christopher kept Randall's metaphor in mind. He didn't relax—it was impossible to, between worrying about Linda, and wondering what the hell the true reason for the loss in communications was—but he fell into a rhythm that allowed him to take note of more of his surroundings. There seemed to be many instances of fire in the surrounding undergrowth, but none that had spread beyond the immediate source. He would have expected one spark would have set off a chain of wildfires, but there was no sign of it. Almost as if something squelched the fires before they could flare.

When they stopped for a brief break he edged closer to Randall. "Do you see that?" Christopher murmured, pointing to the remains of a tree. "It doesn't make sense. This whole area should be nothing but ash."

Before Randall could respond, Kolby shot them a hard look and gave the signal to head out.

Not long after, Samson's red light lit up.

Kolby's hand rose in a signal and all the soldiers took cover, their weapons raised as their eyes tracked the sky. Christopher scrambled after the lieutenant, crouching out of the way in the cover of a scorched bush nearby. He looked up, but all he saw were clouds drifting with the wind. On the other side of Kolby, Samson worked with focused intensity, adjusting and readjusting the settings on his machine until the green light reengaged.

Some of the tension in the group eased and Kolby gave the signal to proceed.

When Christopher tried to climb from hiding, the brambles caught in his clothes and some his flesh. Wincing as he struggled with the thorns, he forgot to watch his feet, to move careful. He cried out as he fell, his foot slipping on something smooth and rounded. The air rushed out of him as he hit the ground hard. Any breath he had left caught in his chest as he pushed himself up.

Blackened bone rested beneath his hand, but that was not what shook him to his core. Glittering between two ribs was a deformed novelty pin. He could almost make out the heat-distorted words *"I'm #2!"*. Or maybe that was his mind filling in the gaps he knew were there.

He was too shocked to cry out, but tears stung his lips on their way down his face. His throat rippled as his stomach heaved. He turned his head hard to the side so the vomit spattered the bushes and not the human remains strewn beneath him. With effort he got himself under control. Swiping his mouth across his uniform sleeve, Christopher reached down a trembling hand to clear away the ash from the fried radio frequency tags draped beside the blackened skull.

He read the first etched line: PIERCE, LINDA, and he could read no more. He knew why Command had lost communication with the practical testing group, and it wasn't because *they* had gone rogue. All the signs pointed to it, only Christopher hadn't known to make those connections before this grim discovery. The self-energizing drone he had helped create was responsible for the isolated fires in the area. It was also a killer. A cold, unfeeling killer, unable to distinguish between humans and an acceptable energy-conversion source. Because they hadn't thought to tell it how. Because *he* hadn't thought to tell it how.

Christopher's earlier pride turned to ashes in his mouth.

He looked up and met Kolby's furious gaze. Christopher didn't give a damn.

"We're here because the military lost communication with the testing facility."

The lieutenant didn't respond.

"They lost communications because everyone's *dead*."

Nothing.

"We have to destroy it," Christopher said.

Kolby glared down at him. "Destroy it? We're here to *retrieve* that valuable piece of military hardware. Now get up and get moving, or we leave you here."

At Kolby's words, Christopher went dead cold as he realized what the military intended.

More than lingering vomit left his mouth sour.

Not knowing what else to do, Christopher reached out and took Linda's pin and her tags, and stowing them in his bag. Only then did he scramble to his feet and fall back in line, hands clutching the straps of the rucksack containing his tablet computer. His mind was a jumble, leaping from one detail to the next, making unexpected connections as only an engineer's could.

A plan took loose form as they made their way closer to the military's practical testing facility.

Maybe facility was the wrong word; the place was a fortress. Shielded walls, (formerly) electrified gate, security doors half a foot thick. To all appearances, the place was better defended than the proverbial Fort Knox. Or it had been.

Christopher had no clue how many personnel had been stationed here, but the piles of scorched bone dotting the courtyard brought bile to his throat, even without counting them. When they made it to the entrance, the soldiers took up a defensive circle around Kolby as he entered a code into the security pad. As he waited, Christopher noted scorch marks along the walls, mostly concentrated around the light stanchions. They were shielded, but the hardest hit had failed, leaving shattered glass on the courtyard below, glittering like smoky diamonds among the ash. In places, the shielding had melted away, leaving fused circuits and slagged wiring exposed.

Christopher's mind recalled Randall's stealth metaphor and made another unanticipated leap, his plan gaining cohesion.

The security door opened and they scrambled inside. Or most of them did. Behind them a beam of laser light shot down from above, catching Samson. The tracker-slash-monitor he'd carried across the wilds smashed down on the marble courtyard as the soldier ignited too quickly to even scream. Christopher stared on in horror as a piece of the sky came down and sucked the energy out of the flame until it guttered out, leaving a fresh pile of scorched bones among the others.

"Secure that door! Move it!" Kolby ordered the remaining men.

Christopher just turned and stared at the lieutenant, shaking his head at Kolby's lack of regard.

Kolby stared back in a challenge that Christopher didn't understand.

"Time to do your job, James." Kolby ordered, breaking the heavy silence. "Get up into that control room and bring that bird down nice and easy so we can get it back to Command."

Only an extreme effort of will kept Christopher's jaw from dropping in outrage. Kolby had in no way acknowledged the loss of Samson. When had men become throw-away commodities? Without a word, Christopher turned away and headed in the direction Kolby had pointed, stopping only to pick up the rucksack he hadn't realized he'd dropped. Randall stood beside it.

Christopher met his eye and saw a kindred resolve in the soldier's gaze. That could have been any of their bones gracing the courtyard.

"Don't worry," Randall said as he reached down and shouldered the bag, "I got your back."

They exchanged the subtlest of nods before they both climbed the stairs to the control room, but Christopher said nothing until the door closed behind them, blocking out the sound of Kolby shouting orders below.

In the sudden silence, Christopher scrambled to connect his tablet computer to the local network, knowing he likely only had a short time before Kolby or one of the others came bursting in to...*supervise.*

"Randall," Christopher called out as he waited for his system to boot up. "I need you to guard the door, buy me some more time."

"What are you doing?"

"Making sure my life's work doesn't become my life's shame," Christopher answered. "That drone needs to be taken out. It's like a vicious dog, turned on its owner. You put the dog down the first time, you don't wait to see if it does it again."

Randall went silent a moment, as if deciding what he should or shouldn't say. "They tried that already, the testing group, before Command ordered them to desist."

"Fuck Command!"

Randall look startled at Christopher's uncharacteristic outburst. Christopher hung his head, shaking it slowly from side to side. "That's my dog. I made it. I'm responsible for…" his throat closed on the words that would haunt him until his dying day. "…every person that beast killed to keep itself in the air. Every one of them…what is it you call it? Friendly fire. I can't make up for that, but I sure as hell can put that dog down. I built the thing! I know it inside and out, I sure as hell know where the kill switch is…I just need the time to flip it."

Randall nodded sharply, then headed for the door. Trusting him, Christopher turned back to his computer, fingers skittering over the keys so fast even he could barely distinguish the individual clicks. Kill switch had been too generous a term, the military would have never authorized such a thing, but most engineers in research and development planned contingencies, just in case everything unexpectedly went to hell.

Christopher heard shouting out in the corridor but tuned it out as he overrode the drone's autonomous systems to take control of the inboard lasers, retracting them into their protective default position. He then shut down the safety protocols to activate those lasers, frying the delicate inner workings and igniting the nylon skin. For the briefest of moments Christopher's "dog" fed off itself before the system red-lined and the drone crashed to the cobbles below, sending a noxious black cloud up into the sky.

As the door to the control room burst open, Christopher hung his head, a single tear falling on the keys as he hit his personal kill switch, wiping his computer hard drive.

"What did you do?"

Straightening, Christopher turned and gave Kolby a hard look.

"I corrected the mistake I never should have made."

Christopher James walked right past Lieutenant Kolby and left the fortress, heading the opposite direction from where they'd left the transport, the memory of Linda Pierce's remains haunting his every step.

THE LAST MAN ON EARTH

Jody Lynn Nye

THE DNA TEST PRINTOUT GLOWED FROM THE SLAB IN OMO PIENAAR'S hands. The female technician regarded him with sympathy. Such a good-looking man! He was of medium height, with broad shoulders that made him look shorter, a slim waist, tightly curled black hair above an almost golden, perfectly oval face, a thin, aquiline nose, strong jaw, and those eyes! Dark blue under long eyelids with a fan of brown-black lashes at the corners. She wished she had better news to give him.

"What this tells you, Mr. Pienaar, are the myriad sources of your genetic material. It's quite remarkable, when you think about it. Gene splicing is still a very young science, but you have more than sixteen animal species, five plant species, a few fungi, and some recombinant DNA that had to be a custom job for your genome." The technician, a middle-aged woman with a bun of white hair yet not a line on her face, whistled in appreciation. "But you are very healthy, I have to say. If I had seen your DNA before I met you, I'd have thought… well, you're nearly perfect, really. May we have your permission to retain your samples? We would love to continue our studies. We will copy you in on any findings we make."

"Yes, all right," Omo said, looking bemused. "What does this mean? For me and my wives?" The old-fashioned term made the technician fix him with a hard stare, but was it really any of her business? That was what Tera and Kyi wanted him to call them. They had admitted him into their coupledom as a full partner only recently, not without a lot of wooing on his part. They were a family.

"It means," the tech said, her expression rueful, "your cells aren't compatible with normal human beings—I'm sorry. I mean, nonmodified humans. I don't really understand how your parents managed to produce a child, but there you are."

"And my sister," Omo added, his voice faint.

The technician raised her eyebrow. "Has she had children?"

"No."

She nodded, and rose to her feet. "I'm so sorry. I can recommend a good consulting geneticist who might be able to help you splice your genetics to create an embryo, but my colleagues and I have run over six hundred thousand computer simulations. All of them came back negative for a natural or even *in vitro* conception. Good luck. I'm so sorry," she repeated, but Omo scarcely heard it as he shuffled toward the door. It slid aside with a hushed hiss like a whispered apology.

Everyone felt sorry for him, but what good did that do?

The perfectly clean streets of the city felt unreal, more like a computer simulation, as he went out to the transportation point. Obediently, he lined up with the passengers waiting for the next hovershuttle, but just as it pulled up, he got out of line, waving them forward. The blue rectangle swept them all away, leaving him the only person left on the street. The only person in the city. The only one in the world. Even the faces behind the silvered glass in the buildings he walked past were no better than images.

He came to the end of the street at the piled, jagged granite boulders that kept vehicles from running off into the river. His apartment—their apartment, now—was part of the steel-blue colored, two-hundred story megaloplex rising on the other side. He ought to walk one block uptown to catch the ferry, or two downtown for the underground. It was too far, and he didn't want to be around anyone else, maybe never again. The torment roiled his belly so much he couldn't stand it any longer.

To hell with it.

Omo stripped off his jacket and tied it around his waist. He clambered up onto the rocks and stuffed his shoes into his shirt.

Below, the fast-moving current slapped against the bank. A bright green wrapper swept past him and away. Never mind. Omo leaned over, his arms raised behind him.

"No!" a woman's voice shrieked out.

Omo didn't hear the syllables that followed. His dive took him into the current with hardly a splash.

Beneath the water, the city was nothing more than wavering shadows. His webbed toes and long reach, inheritances from an ancestor who wanted to compete for Olympic gold, propelled him almost as fast as the school of silver minnows he had just surprised.

The cold of the water shocked him out of his mood. Omo wanted to blame *someone* for his predicament. His parents had done what humans had for centuries: had sex, conceived, given birth, for themselves, never thinking what the modifications Mother had had to reduce the tendency for glaucoma in her family, nor Father's splicing nerve and tendon genes that made him the most nimble judo-ka on the entire North American continent, might mean for their children. It seemed, he thought glumly, recalling every detail of the analysis with photographic perfection, as if every ancestor stretching back sixteen generations to the 21st century had made some kind of change to their DNA. Some did it to save their lives, like Great-great-grandfather Feldman, who had Tay-Sachs disease. Others did it to make their babies match their plastic surgery, like Marie Suh, his fourth great-grandmother on his mother's side. Was that small nose really worthwhile? But had any of them thought about what the changes they were making would mean for the future?

Obviously not. They had only thought of themselves, and he was the one who had to pay for that. If it wasn't for the possibility of a technological intervention, he could not possibly engender children. If he *was* the last man on Earth, he would literally *be* the last man on Earth. The human race would halt with him.

I'm the end of my line. The thought affected Omo so strongly that he stopped in the middle of the channel. He looked up through twilight-dark water. If he expelled the breath in his enhanced lungs, he would surely have the strength to push up to the surface to draw another—but did he want to? What was the use? Who cared if he survived? He could drown right there, and put an end to the disappointment that stabbed him in the belly. He exhaled hard.

Blackness threatened the edges of his vision, and his extremities started to feel the water's cold. His bloodstream had made use of all the available oxygen, bonding it into CO_2. Of their own volition, his feet kicked upward, pushing him toward the air. He lay upon the face of the river, letting it bear him downstream, as he gasped in long, rasping breaths. Life persisted. Whether or not he could produce more of his kind, he was a living organism. But that wasn't enough.

"Hey, citizen!"

A spotlight hit him. He held up a hand as the actinic beam pierced his eyeballs to the back of his skull. Strong hands grasped him and pulled him onto a hard surface that smelled like marine epoxy and bleach. A fleshy, pale-skinned female with a badge on the breast of her high-visibility yellow slicker regarded him with worried, bulbous eyes. She had four arms, with suckers on her slender palms and wrists. Part octopus, Omo guessed.

"Are you all right?"

"I'm fine," he assured her. He pulled himself up and sat on one of the molded fiberglass seats along the side of the boat. She helped steady him. One of her hands wound its way into each of his pockets, until it came up with his ID. Another hand snaked up to scan it with a portable reader that flashed red.

"We got a report of a jumper matching your description." She glanced down at his feet. "Guess there wasn't anything to worry about, Omo Pienaar. Can I take you anywhere?"

"I was just crossing the river," he said, nodding toward the shining, blue building, now lit up by streetlights and ornamental spotlights. "My apartment is over there."

"No problem. Marnie, west bearing 45°."

"Aye, sir," the mechanical voice of the rescue boat said. Omo wrung out his jacket and put it over his lap. The lifeboat operator handed him a worn yellow towel. He used it to dry off his feet and put his shoes back on. The boat thrummed over the rippling water. The pilot manipulated the controls with her multiple hands, perfectly at home in her environment.

"Do you have kids, captain?" Omo asked.

"Yeah, two. Both of them are in high school. Why do you ask?"

"We want to have kids," he said, not wanting to share his pain. That part was true, anyhow.

She threw back her head and laughed. "Don't hurry, citizen. I got pregnant while I was completing my training. Had to stow them in an artificial womb. Missed half the fun."

Omo had to grin, even if it hurt.

The captain steered her craft to the jetty nearest his apartment complex and let him off onto the wet plascrete stairs.

"You be careful now," she said, with a sympathetic look. "You've got your life to live."

"Who's there?" Tera called from the bedroom.

"Me," Omo said, a little disappointed. He had hoped he had beaten both of them home so he could clean up in private. The main door slid shut and sealed behind him.

"Lovebird!" she said, rushing out and throwing her arms around him. Her cuddlesome curves fit comfortingly against him. He embraced her warmly, but she flinched back. "You're all wet. What happened?"

"I… decided to swim instead of taking the shuttle."

"Oh. I didn't think it was that nice out. But you don't feel the cold, do you?"

"Not much," he said, not wanting to blame Great-grandfather Hiroki for *that* change, incorporating ptarmigan DNA into their genome so he could explore the Antarctic. "How was teaching?"

Her round face lit up. "Great! This batch of kids really absorbs knowledge. About half of them have some kind of educational modification, so I can really get into the history of art as well as technique. The others…" She shook her head, making her shoulder-length dreadlocks dance, then stopped to study him. "What's the matter? What did the doctors say?"

"Let's wait until Kyi comes home, all right?" he pleaded.

Kyi, Tera's co-wife, was a whirlwind presence. The very ground always seemed to shake when she entered a room, like a friendly earthquake. She dwarfed both of them by several centimeters and a dozen or more kilograms. She had risen from being a carpenter to running the construction firm that had employed her. Her northern-European heritage showed in her long, broad bones, thick golden hair, and slanted eyes like Omo's. He had lusted after her since he had first seen her, then been overwhelmed by the sweet nature of her partner. How lucky that they were already a committed pair. Was it just biological imperative that had attracted him to them? The urge to combine his genes with theirs? Angrily, he pushed the thought aside. There was no use speculating.

"What's wrong?" Kyi asked, releasing them from her embrace. Her intuition was as good as telepathy. She searched his face.

"He saw the geneticists today," Tera explained, fussing around them both. She fluffed a cushion before Kyi settled down against it. "He wouldn't tell me what was in the report."

"Let's see it," Kyi said, putting out an imperious palm. Her head-of-the-family tone brooked no disagreement. Omo ducked his head and held out his slab as if he was a schoolboy handing over a bad report card. Kyi read with staccato flicks of her eyes. Her astonishing speed and retention had also been the result of a genetic alteration. Tera read over her shoulder, going a little slower. "Great Mother! Well, the fish wasn't much of a surprise. You are more at home in the water than on land. Did you even suspect the rest of this?"

"No," Omo said. He flung himself out of his chair and walked to the wall. Tera clicked her tongue in concern.

"What's the matter? You've got some cool stuff going on here. Between us, we'll make some pretty babies."

"No," Omo said, resting his head against the cool, painted surface. "We won't."

"What do you mean?" Tera said, sounding frightened. "Are you... are you breaking up with us?"

He spun. Tera had her hands clasped tightly. Kyi rose from her chair, peering at him with tears starting in her eyes. Omo wanted to fold them both in his arms, but he felt too sick to move.

"Not me. But you might want to break up with me. You didn't read the last page of the report. I can't breed with anyone."

"Are you... sterile?" Kyi asked.

"What's the difference? I'm not even the same species as you! My genetics are so mixed up that the tech just stopped short of calling me a freak. My DNA won't combine with yours, not *in utero* or *in vitro*. So, I'll understand if you don't want me around any longer. I'll release you from our vows."

The hurt in his voice brought Tera right across the room. She held him tight against her soft bosom. He wanted to sink into her flesh and never come out again.

"You're not a freak."

"Why all the melodrama?" Kyi asked, raising her pale brows. "It's not the end of the world."

"It is of mine."

"Bah! Male attitude! That's not the only reason we love you." Something in his expression made her frown. "Is that all? Is it all that we are to you? Breeding females?"

Tera released him and stepped back into Kyi's sheltering arm. Omo felt as if he had been punched in the belly.

"No! But… it was part of our plans, to have children. We want babies. Wanted."

"We'll cope," Kyi said, firmly. "Somehow. Right, Tera?"

The smaller woman hesitated.

"Well," she said. "I'll have to think about that. Could you… have some of the genetic changes reversed? So *in vitro* would work?"

Omo would have done anything to take that frightened look off her face.

"I'll try," he promised.

Within his family, he gladly followed Kyi's lead. Outside, he was known for being a take-charge individual. His employers at the design engineering consultancy never hesitated to turn him loose on a difficult project. His grasp of problem-solving—undoubtedly enhanced by some six-times ancestor—allowed him to focus intently on specific details and analyze them out to multiple conclusions he could consider simultaneously.

He set his personal computer on a comprehensive search while he went about his tasks of the day. With difficulty, he ignored the gleaming black slab propped up on his clear glass desk as three-dimensional images flashed up and turned in mid-air. At last, the search stopped, displaying the name Gene-ius Corp, Inc., located in South Africa. When Omo had finished with his final client of the day, he secured the sliding door of his office, then logged into the queue for his chosen technical geneticist, a transwoman named Mars Delgaro, who proudly displayed the images of her three biological children on her website. Her family looked happy and healthy. The sight gave Omo hope.

Half of his office disappeared as the hologram of her office formed. Brilliant sunshine streamed through ornamental oriel windows. Delgaro did not sit at a desk, but in an easy chair carved of shining chestnut-colored wood. She had on a dark blue skirt suit that showed off long, very shapely legs, crossed at the knees. Like Kyi, she was large-boned and strong-jawed, but no other traces of her male birth were evident.

"Do you have my file there?" he asked, once they had greeted one another.

"I certainly do, Mr. Pienaar," Delgaro said, holding up the slab from her lap. Her voice had a slight nasal twang. "And thank you for choosing Gene-ius. But I don't understand what it is you want us to do."

Omo set his jaw.

"I thought my AIssistant made that clear. I want you to undo the genetic changes that my ancestors made. Change me back to the way my line was supposed to be."

Delgaro frowned at the slab. Statistics with which Omo had become all too familiar over a long and sleepless night scrolled up on the air beside her.

"As you may know, sir, some of the genetic engineering that was done in previous generations, especially 150 years ago, was irresponsibly kack-handed. No one paid attention to the side effects of adding specific genes or altering chromosomes. It was all done so crudely, but our ancestors didn't have the technology we do. We deal with subtleties now. I believe that you've seen from our catalog how we have satisfied our clients. Small details are within our grasp. I've been a Gene-ius patient myself. I wasn't born with a womb or ovaries, but I have them now, fully functional. My children were born healthy."

"That's what I want!" Omo said, the words rushing out of him. "Can you do what my wives suggested? Alter my genes so I'm… I'm normal?"

Delgaro hesitated.

"Well, Mr. Pienaar, I wish we could. Do you have records of the unaltered genomes of all your ancestors, so we can determine exactly what changes were made when?"

"No. But you can see my DNA now. Can you remove the lizard genes, or the fish genes, or plants?"

She shook her head, making her long, blonde hair dance.

"Mr. Pienaar, you can't unring a bell."

"Well, why not? You can add genes. I know you can subtract them. Go ahead and do it! I can be in South Africa in two days!"

"Sir, I can't."

"Why can't you? You're supposed to be the best in the world at genetic manipulation!"

"Without modesty," she said, "we *are*. But the first law of medicine is to do no harm. Those changes were made in order to enhance your ancestors' lives. What records you do have show that some of these alterations were made to cure harmful or fatal conditions. To return you to the state of your ancestors' vulnerability would be irresponsible."

"True," Omo said, thoughtfully. "All right. Leave those alone."

The specialist leaned back in her chair, reading more of the extract.

"…Others were added as enhancements, true, but all of them have been beneficial." She looked up and met his eyes. "I read this carefully when it came in, but I'm reviewing it. Just *which* conditions do you want me to undo? Your amazing stamina? Your strength? Eyesight? Your intelligence? All of these are desirable characteristics, not flaws."

"But… they are preventing me from exercising my right as a living being, that of reproducing a new generation."

Delgaro shook her head. "Seriously, I can't guarantee that reversing any of these characteristics would achieve what you hope for. I understand your frustration, really I do. We can't change you in ways that will diminish you. For one thing, that would be against the law. You're healthy, more than functional. People would die to be what you are. Anything we did would be considered damage, not restoration."

"But I can't be a father!" Omo wailed. His voice echoed off the ceiling of his office.

The tech was silent for a moment, then lifted her chin resolutely. "Neither can millions of your fellow men, sir. Some of them are simply sterile. Others have lost the ability to produce viable sperm through disease or injury. We help them, either by creating a fetus by combining their cells and their partners', or finding someone whose DNA structure complements theirs. In your case, we couldn't guarantee the results, as your other geneticist told you. We also offer therapy, and encourage them to foster or adopt. Have you considered either of those possibilities?"

The silence was oppressive on Omo's side of the room. The technician pursed her lips.

"I see. I have met many men and women like you."

"Not like me!"

"Yes, just like you. Your offspring must be the product of your own body."

"You did it. You advertise your own success on your website! It's one of the reasons I came to you."

"You're absolutely right," Delgaro said, tilting her head. "*I* was like you. When I transitioned, I longed to give birth to my partner's children. We were lucky enough to succeed with two, but we were proud to adopt our youngest child, and we're petitioning to adopt another soon. Permit me to say that is very selfish of you not to consider it, when so many children desperately need loving homes."

Omo felt his face grow hot as his ire rose. What a hypocrite!

"I can see I have wasted my time speaking to you!" he snapped.

Delgaro shook her head sadly. "No, no, you haven't. I wish I had better news for you. I can't change your situation without altering you so thoroughly that it would change the rest of your life. You need to know that. But we are doing genetic studies. If you want, you can be a part of them. We can try splicing, one gene at a time, although you'll have to sign a waiver holding us harmless. If we end up not being able to help you personally, what we do together will offer answers for future generations to come."

"Not mine," Omo growled. Before the tech could speak, he waved his hand. The communication link closed, and the hologram vanished.

He slammed his hand down on the glass, making his slab clatter. He *knew* he was being shallow. Deep within himself, he felt the overwhelming need to have his own child. The thought of not being able to create a life made his guts twist in frustration. To have parenthood denied to him hurt at a fundamental level that he would never, as a loving, accepting man of society, have believed himself capable. He hated himself for that. Delgaro was right, curse her.

Another part of his frustration was how his functional sterility would affect his wives. He had been hurt beyond measure when Tera showed her dismay for his condition. He couldn't help it, damn it!

He fell back in his chair and stared at the smooth, beige ceiling. He ought to leave and go home, but he couldn't face Tera or Kyi again without answers. Home would remind him every minute that their union would never be complete, the way they wanted it to be.

"AIssistant," he said. The holo rose from the small black slab. "Go to the second choice on the list. We'll find someone who can make this work."

His eyes and his throat were dry and raw by the time he finished the sixteenth interview. Not one of the leading geneticists around the globe had the skills to fix him. A couple dismissed him rudely when he tried to insist on treatment. Others were sympathetic but sad that they couldn't help him, like Delgaro. In the hour before dawn, he finally gave up and took a late shuttle home.

Kyi was a light sleeper. She woke up when he crept into their bedroom and flipped back the corner of the coverlet on his side of the bed. She lifted a beckoning finger, then pointed at Tera, who lay soundly asleep in Kyi's other arm.

Omo crawled onto the soft padding and nestled against her soft, warm frame. He set his hand on her rib cage, running his finger along the lower curve of her full breast.

"I'm sorry," he whispered. "I was trying to fix this."

"I know," Kyi murmured, with a gentle smile that wrenched his heart. She hugged his slim body to hers and kissed the top of his head. "We guessed, so we didn't call. Tera left dinner for you, but I said you wouldn't be hungry. Sleep. You need it."

Omo gave a heavy sigh and breathed in her sweet essence. *I don't deserve them*, he thought. But he slept.

His AI hadn't found him any other specialists to talk to by the time he woke, an inadequate three hours from climbing into bed. The three of them showered together, then Tera brought out a fragrant hot casserole for their breakfast. It was her own recipe, Omo's favorite. He caught her hand and kissed her palm.

"Thank you," he said. She drew the palm along his cheek. Her warm, brown eyes were sad only for a moment, then she bent to dish out a hearty portion for him.

"Eat up," she said, pushing the plate across the tabletop to him. "I have a *long* day ahead. The kids have to present three examples of poetry and read one of their own poems."

Kyi shook her head. "*Brr*! I'd sooner dig ditches."

Tera laughed. "I know!"

Omo watched them. Usually, he joined in the banter, but that morning he felt like an outsider all over again.

Unnervingly, Kyi caught his discomfort with that intuition of hers. She gave him a fierce hug.

"Don't worry!" she said. "It's still us three, forever."

But wouldn't four or five be better? he thought, as he gathered up his slab and coat to go out.

With his sophisticated debugging software, Omo hardly needed to pay attention to the security program he had designed for his current client's mainframe. If the computer stopped to ask him for a solution or resolve a contradiction, he responded, but it still left too much time for his mind to wander.

Five days had passed since the devastating diagnosis. He had to find another outlet for his passion and energy. If there would be no tiny footsteps, no child that looked like him sharing smiles and confidences, no future for his line, then what was there to live for? He thought he was a modern human, but the primitive animal was still inside him, and not that far below the surface. Omo was ashamed. He couldn't help it any more than he could control the need to eat or sleep or excrete. Maybe that fellow who had cyberjacked himself into an android body had the right idea. Give up your body altogether, then genetics no longer matter.

Ah, but then he wouldn't have the pleasure of feeling soft flesh under his hands, or the taste of a loved one's mouth. No matter how lifelike an artificial body was, it wasn't human.

But was he? Omo sat up as the realization hit him. He had been bred to be something new.

"AIssistant, new document, private, voice-locked, two columns."

"Yes, sir? Title?"

"Continuation or cessation. No…" He hesitated, running his tongue over his lips. They felt dry and coarse. "Traits, positive and negative."

"Yes, sir. Ready."

With this list, he could identify characteristics that he would be willing to give up to be able to breed as a human being. Breathlessly, Omo spooled out all of the benefits of his enhanced genetics. Superior healing, the ability to hold his breath for nearly an hour, his enhanced eyesight, dense musculature. The immunity to certain diseases, including Tay-Sachs. Youthfulness and smooth skin, bestowed by the king cobra fragment. Excellent coordination, owing to natural talent, but surely including the capuchin monkey genes. Affinity for the water, that smooth-hound shark bestowed. Longevity, tortoise genes.

Handsomeness—well, who was to say how much actually existed in his family line before the donor genes were added, or what the result would be if he spliced them out? His putative child could have a deviated septum, or some other inherited hazard. No matter how he searched, he couldn't locate an image of Great-grandmother Marie before she had had her surgery.

He wasn't surprised by the lengthy list of positives. What did take him aback was that he couldn't find a single negative trait that was easy to pinpoint. Everything had been done to enhance his genetic line, resulting in chimeras. Him. His sister.

"Open a communication to Nira," he told AIssistant.

"Yes, sir."

He couldn't help but be moved by the perfect image that rose from his black slab. Athletic, slim, long neck, oval face, smooth, ageless skin. His sister had all the same physical traits he did, but her long eyes shone with an emerald gleam.

"I knew you would call," she said, with a laugh that held a trace of bitterness. "Kyi called me days ago."

"Did you know we were… chimeras?" he said.

She nodded. "I wanted to have a child years ago. I signed onto a donor registry. They never could find me a compatible mate, of either sex."

Omo glared. "Why didn't you tell *me?*"

She glared back. "Because I hoped you were different! It hurt so much, I couldn't admit it to myself, let alone you. I thought you would tease me, and I couldn't take that. I'm sorry. I've had a lot of therapy since then. I was going to call you soon. Not that it would have cushioned the blow. It's horrible, isn't it?"

"Yes," Omo said. "I'm sorry. I'll… I'll talk with you later."

"Don't do anything stupid!"

"Why would you say such a thing?" he demanded.

'Because I thought about it, back then. I've had a lot of help. You should find someone to talk with. Don't hurt yourself. I love you, you idiot. Stay alive. We're pretty awesome the way we are, you know."

Then she hung up.

The pain twisted in Omo's belly. So she had also thought about killing herself. His mind stopped there and wouldn't move any farther. Why continue? Nira wanted him to see a shrink. He gave a bitter laugh.

I would rather die than whine to another human being about my problem.

The idea stayed in the back of his mind during the rest of the morning.

Instead of sending out for lunch, he astonished his co-workers by leaving the building.

"I need some air," he told them.

He took a cash-cab for kilometers to the edge of town. A dark-web search had turned up a pharmacy that would compound drugs, no questions asked.

"You want a muscle-relaxant?" the big woman in the consulting cubicle asked him.

"I assume we're being recorded?" Omo asked, looking up at the corners of the tiny room. It smelled antiseptically clean, in contrast to its appearance, which was shabby in the extreme.

"Hell, no, citizen. You want to tell me what you want it for, and why you won't ask your own medical system for it?"

He touched his shoulder. "The tension is so painful I can't sleep." That much was true. "I need it to rest. My doctor doesn't take me seriously."

She narrowed her small, piggy eyes at him. "We don't assist in homicides, you know. That would get us all a trip to the repro-grammer."

"No! It's for me. I swear it is."

"Ninety credits. You wait here."

The wall behind her opened, and her chair slid back into the recess, shutting Omo alone in the room. His hands tingled. What was he doing?

I am solving a problem, he told himself firmly. *I'll swim home tonight. Somewhere… in the middle, I'll use the drug, and I won't save myself. When the rescue boat comes for me, I'll already have drowned. Painless. Tragic accident. Easy. Over.*

With the syringe in his pocket, he returned to the office. He felt an odd sense of comfort, almost cheerfulness, having the answer to his overwhelming tension at hand. Kyi and Tera would find someone else who would become the mate he couldn't be.

He counted down the hours until he would go to the water's edge and dive in. Three to go. Two. Should he record a message to his wives, telling them goodbye? No, then they would know he had done it on purpose.

The last hour clicked up on the chronometer. Methodically, Omo arranged the files in his computer, with addresses to send them to his fellow employees to take over each of his clients. He refused to leave any personal effects in his office that anyone else would have to deal with. He was amazed at how clear-headed he felt. The zen of the moment refreshed him. He almost felt as though the drug would be a release from the misery that had dogged him for days. The childless man would disappear as though he had never been.

AIssisant interrupted the silence.

"Visitors, sir."

Omo almost startled. "Who? I have no appointments."

"Your wives, sir. Kyi Pienaar and Tera Pienaar."

The shock rendered him silent. He had not intended to see them again.

He stood up behind his tidied desk as the door opened. Both of the women beamed at him. Kyi bore down on him like an advancing steamroller.

"There you are!" she said cheerfully. She wrapped him in a bone-crushing hug.

"What… what are you doing here?" Omo asked, holding himself stiff in her grasp.

Tera looked up at him, a mischievous glint in her warm brown eyes.

"We have a surprise for you."

"Come on," Kyi said. She picked up his slab, then took his coat from the hook behind the door and draped it over her arm. Omo wanted to scramble and take the jacket away from her, lest she find the syringe in the pocket. Tera took him by the hand and pulled him toward the lift.

"He's leaving early today," she told his colleague, Vera Salomon.

"No problem!" Vera said. She waved and went back to her own work.

A private shuttle waited at the door. Tera let go and hopped into the passenger seat. Kyi pushed Omo into the back and jumped in after him. The door closed, and the shuttle moved silently into the stream of traffic.

"Where are we going?" he asked, feeling as though he was being kidnapped. Had they read his mind? Kyi's intuition sometimes scared him.

"You'll see," Tera said.

Twenty minutes later, they pulled up in front of the geneticist's laboratory. Kyi pushed him out of the cab and into the lift. Both women stared at the advancing numbers over the door.

"They can't help me. I've been through this!"

"Patience!" Kyi insisted. "No more questions. It's a surprise."

They dragged him out of the elevator, but not toward the door of the consultant geneticist. Instead, they brought him into an office where couples, triads, and a few happy-looking singles were waiting. When the receptionist spotted Kyi, she beckoned her over. Tera waited with Omo while Kyi held a whispered conversation.

Omo fretted, fingering the syringe in his pocket. He had steeled himself. It made him impatient to postpone the inevitable. Then, a very tall man, taller than Kyi, came out of a doorway and beckoned them into a treatment room.

"Now, citizens," he said, sitting down on a rolling stool. "I'm Dr. Parker. I'll take care of you all the way through the process. I know you will be very relieved to have a happy outcome. We will do our best to make certain that happens. Both of you ladies have checked through as healthy, and the cells are prepared and waiting."

"Doctor, we haven't told him yet," Tera said, blushing a little. "Would you give us privacy for a moment?"

He smiled. "I'll be just outside the door."

"Kyi, what is going on here?" Omo asked. She took his hands.

"We can't have children, not in the normal way," Kyi said. "Not even in the abnormal way. But we can have children if we clone you."

"Clones?" Omo asked.

"Yes," Kyi said, her smile almost smug. "You may not be compatible with us, but you're compatible with *yourself*. Say the word, and we'll both have your children. *Our* children."

Omo was speechless.

"They'll both be… me. With nothing of you in them."

"We'll be giving birth to them," Kyi said. She patted her belly as if a child already grew there. "We three are the only parents they will ever have."

"Say the word," Tera urged him, her soul in her eyes. "You are not only your genes. We love you, the real you."

"They're going to be beautiful," Kyi assured him. "They probably won't look exactly like you, you know. You've got plenty of recessives bumping around in there. Maybe they'll look like a ptarmigan."

Tera laughed.

Omo worked his mouth, overwhelmed by happiness and worry in equal parts.

"But they won't be able to find mates," he said.

Kyi shrugged.

"So we're kicking the can down the road one more generation. Perhaps by then, we'll find someone whose genetics match our children's. With the billions of people in the world, someone's will surely recombine to a compatible mix. If not this generation, then the next. In the meantime, we are still a family."

"Say yes," Tera begged him. "The doctor is going to come back soon. Please say yes."

Omo embraced his loves, almost unable to breathe for joy.

"Yes," he said.

On their way out of the building, Omo threw the syringe in the nearest disposer chute.

CHASING THE BALL

Peter Prellwitz

Earth date: Monday, September 22, 2245 AD
Martian date: Tujun 19, 104 MD
98 Astronomical Units from Earth

"Subspace field construction is complete and stable." Chief Engineer Mahlon Stewart's voice came over the comlink, steady and sure. Pam cocked her head slightly. There seemed to be an undertone of worry she wasn't used to hearing from Mal. "Fusion engines at full, running point zero five one light speed."

"Acknowledged, Chief. Prime singularity feed for mass insertion into the subspace matrix," Captain Tessler replied calmly. He turned to his left, toward Pam, the *Horizon's* First Officer. "Ship's status, if you please, Carlson."

She glanced at her station holopanels even though she had just done so.

"We're in the black, Captain," she said crisply. "All departments on continuous reporting. No alerts; no…" A blue indicator came up. "Correction, sir. We have a fluctuation in the secondary gravity plating on…"

"Where?" Tessler barked, interrupting Pam and wasting a precious second.

"Priming singularity feed," Mal reported. "Light speed available in ten seconds."

"Upper port side, sir, two meters above and left of Spike Six." She tapped quickly on the panel floating in front of her. "Increasing adjacent plating fields to compensate." She frowned at the results. "Captain, the fields are holding but there is still fluctuation." The abort FTL button appeared on her holo, as well as the Captain's. "I recommend abort, sir."

"Singularity feed primed; subspace matrix ready in all respects," Mal said over the com. "Light speed available at your command, Captain."

Captain Tessler paused. He glanced around the bridge, filled with guests and dignitaries, all of them stunned into silence. Even the *homo Marinas* people had a representative. Directly in front, between him and the Pilot/Navigator stations, was a huge holocam, broadcasting the historic event to Earth. Pam's hand hovered over the abort button.

"Engage singularity drive," Tessler ordered.

"Aye, sir," Mal replied. "Creating singularity."

There was no surge of acceleration. Instead, the heavy throb of the fusion engine dropped and was replaced by a rumble deep inside the belly of the *Horizon* as the singularity drive activated.

Pam's panel immediately went bright blue, then flashed to white before burning out. She slammed the Abort FTL, but it had vanished in the burn out.

"Distortion in the subspace matrix. Containment loss!" shouted Ensign Behrens, the pilot.

On the front screen was a view of the massive duranium shield that blocked off all view of space forward the ship. Spikes One, Two, and Six were visible. As they watched, the gravity plating above Six failed and a hole appeared, the singularity at the bows having pulled the failed area into it. In less than two seconds, Spike Six was pulled in. Alarms sounded throughout the bridge.

"Disengage the drive!" Captain Tessler shouted. "Disengage the…"

The duranium shield was stripped and absorbed into the singularity, a pitch-black maw inside the collapsing subspace field. The *Horizon* jerked, then plummeted into the…

"Simulation failed," the ship computer stated as it forced Pam out of her ship's core puterverse link. "Do you wish to reset and attempt a different solution?"

Pam stood up from her desk and shook her head to orient herself. Getting kicked out of the puterverse was like being shocked awake from a nightmare. Still adjusting, she looked around to make sure her cabin was still in one piece. It was. She shook her head again and puffed out a breath, giving a short laugh.

"Whoa."

"Do you wish to reset and attempt a different solution?" the computer repeated.

"No, thanks," Pam replied. The solution was obvious; aborting the light speed attempt was always the solution in every scenario that had a ship malfunction. What wasn't as clear was why, out of thousands of possible scenarios, the computer had chosen this one four times in the past week.

She glanced at the chronometer. Still an hour before she needed to report to the bridge, and nearly three hours until rendezvous with the long-range patrol ship *CJ Kelley*, and at least two more hours until drive activation. Now would be a good time to visit Mal in Engineering. Besides, she had little desire to report to the bridge even a minute before she had to. The bridge was kept at Earth gravity to accommodate the crush of Earth-based reporters and dignitaries present. The majority of the crew being from Mars, including Pam, the other ten decks of the *Horizon*, were kept at 38% Earth gravity; Martian normal.

She left her Deck One quarters and made for the eledisc. The hall was full of crew and visitors along for the journey. This was only the second attempt at faster than light travel — the first one had ended in disaster just three months earlier — yet no one seemed particularly nervous; the excitement of success engulfed the oblivion of failure. The crew had been together over a year now, training while the ship was still being constructed in space dock, so they knew what they were undertaking. All were confident, but all knew the risk. These politicians, corporate hotshots, and reporters on the other hand seemed to own a fearlessness through ignorance. *Not my place to judge*, Pam thought. *And it is probably a risk worth...*

"Commander! Hold, please!"

Pam looked up. Ensign Behrens, the ship's pilot, was calling for her. She'd walked the corridor and gotten on the eledisc without paying attention.

"Sorry, Ensign," she said as he joined her on the energy-planed lift. "Where to?"

"Upper Engineering, ma'am. Deck Five, please." He indicated the tabinal in his left hand. "Final independent flight path verifications from Earth and Mars." The eledisc descended quietly.

"I've done those more than few times over the years, Ensign," Pam commented. She extended her hand. "Mal's in Main Engineering right now. Here, I'll take the report to him." She glanced at it. "They're useless on an FTL ship, especially fifteen billion kilometers outside the Kuiper belt. But back when I was younger than you and piloted the old freighters, a tight flight path meant getting into port earlier, allowing for faster turnaround for the next flight."

"Yes, ma'am." Behrens nodded. "I grew up on the *DL White*. Dad was the pilot and Mom the engineer."

"*Whitey*, huh?" Pam replied, giving a little laugh. "Commander Stewart and I both started on the *McFarland*. We shared a berth with your ship on Luna 31." The eledisc stopped at Deck Five. "We'll catch up later when we're off duty. For now, it's probably best to focus on not vaporizing this ship. Carry on, Ensign."

"I look forward to it, ma'am." He stepped off. "See you on the bridge, Commander."

Pam descended to Deck Seven and got off, thinking pleasant thoughts; perfect for smoothing out the lingering effects of the puterverse kick out.

It was a brief moment only. Engineering occupied the space of three decks in the aft quarter of a ship that was 80 meters long, not counting the massive duranium shield. For the eight months since the ship's crew space had been enclosed and pressurized, Engineering was the place to come and grab a few minutes break from the somewhat cramped places everywhere else. Not so right now. The majority of the press had gone down to Engineering for the one and only scheduled Q&A with Lt. Commander Mahlon Stewart. Already famous—to his chagrin—for his contribution to the enhanced fusion engines that came out of the Troid Piracy War of the previous decade, as well as his hands-on work with the singularity drive of this decade, he was now the Intraplanetary Transit Authority's Fleet Chief Engineer. Pam had been with Mal for twenty-two Earth years, going together from ship to ship, from freighters to combat ships to the *Horizon*. But it didn't take knowing him all that time to tell Mal was not happy.

"So, Commander," a famous puterverse blogalnist asked, "Could you explain how FTL will work in such a way that our viewers will understand?"

"Ship go fast," Mal replied instantly. Pam only just held in a *snerk!* to Mal's answer. Fame had never impressed him.

"Hilarious," came the acidic reply. "All right, then, Commander; how would you explain it to our younger audience? And please, use words they'll understand. Can you do that?"

Pam nodded when Mal's face brightened slightly. Teaching kids was the best way to get a positive reaction from her lanky, taciturn friend.

"Sure can," he replied. "We're going to create a singularity — called a black hole by a lot of people — right in front of the ship's shield. It will form into a perfect sphere, rounder than any planet or moon or ball. It's so small, you can't even see it with the naked eye. But it's still dangerous to everything around it, which is why we have to be so far from the solar system when we create it. To keep the singularity from sucking us into its gravity well, we embed it into a subspace field, which we call a matrix. Subspace is the universe's duct tape. If in doubt, subspace it.

"When the singularity is formed, it compresses space in front of us while pulling us toward it. We don't control the singularity directly. Instead, we control the subspace matrix that surrounds it with the three prongs that go through the forward shield and extend off the ship's bows. So we're kinda pushing the ball-shaped singularity while being pulled by it.

"Once we've gone through the compressed space, it stretches back out behind us. That lets us keep the same time as everyone else while in the field. Otherwise, we'd arrive at a new system in a year for us, but decades for everyone back on Mars." He paused. "I mean Earth. Through adjusting the mass of the singularity and how close it is to the bows, the *Horizon* can increase and decrease the compression, which adjusts velocity, up to a hundred and fifty times faster than the speed of light, relative to normal space. We're only going to push to about forty on this maiden trip, and go about 600 AUs in a couple hours before turning back and dropping off the guests and you guys with the *CJ Kelley*. Then we head for Proxima at about 100 FTL, and get there in a couple weeks."

The press corps had gone silent, causing Pam to smile. Mal told it as simply as possible, but it was still leaving some of them a little stunned.

"That's your explanation for kids?" another pushy reporter called out. Admittedly, Pam thought all reporters were pushy.

Mal shrugged. In his explanation he'd already spoken more words than he normally did in two days. Especially to people he didn't know. Nor particularly liked.

"I think so, yeah. Kids are pretty smart these days."

A different puterverse blogalnist spoke up. "And what's your explanation for the corporate world, especially for the marketing folks who need to explain things as they understand them?"

"Ship go REAL fast."

A combination chuckle, disapproving murmur went up from the crowd. They wanted a story and they weren't going to get it. Time to end this before it went extremely south.

"Excuse me!" Pam shouted, drawing all attention off Mal and onto her. "I'm sorry to end the conference early, but we've just received the final independent flight path verifications from Earth and Mars and need to sequence them to our current configurations. I'm sure you understand how important it is that we have our Chief Engineer work on them immediately."

Having been given a talking down to by Mal, the majority were more than willing to nod sagely, demonstrating that they indeed understood procedure. Holocams began shutting down and there was a general movement toward the elediscs.

"Thank you for your understanding!" Pam shouted gratefully. Only one reporter lingered, then approached Pam. She recognized him as a fellow Martian, someone from the Enla Times.

"Okay, Shin," Pam said to his hopeful look. "Make it quick."

"Thanks, Commander. This is for you. You've been captain of your own ships since mid-95. You've garnered…"

"Since 2228," Pam corrected. "On an ITA ship, we're required to use Terran dating, not Martian." Pam shrugged apologetically. "Though it's nice to hear."

"Sorry. So after seventeen Earth years in command, how's it feel to not be the captain?"

"It's strange I'll admit," Pam replied. "But the opportunity was too good to pass up. And Captain Tessler is far more qualified than I am to command humankind's first FTL ship. It's an honor to serve under him. Besides," she added with a wink, "I get the chair when he's off duty."

"Thanks, Commander," Shin said, giving a quick bow. He gave a knowing grin. "I'll leave you and Commander Stewart to your 'sequencing'."

"Now him I like," Mal said after the reporter had left.

"Me, too. Zhong's one of the good ones. I'll give him some real time after you've not sucked us into a singularity."

"Sure. You and I can sit down with him an' regale the stories. Give him some decent fluff stuff." Mal went back to his holopanels, tickling the virtual controls to gain the precise view he preferred. He gave a short laugh.

"What?" Pam asked, peering at the holographic pane view. It looked to be a zoomed view of Spike Six, one of the immense half-dozen spikes required to bleed off mass as plasma once the *Horizon* needed to drop out of FTL flight. "Something funny?"

"Just your bullshit about the flight path verifications. You were always good at shoveling it to the tagalongs without pissin' them off. That's why you're command and I'm engineering. Engines don't have feelings to hurt. Unless you ignore them."

"As you've told me many times."

He turned and grinned at her. "We're alive, aren't we?"

"How's the gravity plating around Spike Six, Mal?" Pam suddenly asked.

Mal looked back and put the view into diagnostic. With an expertise that came not just from years of experience but also a natural-born affinity for and understanding of the engines of movement, Mal reached a conclusion in ten seconds that would take any other skilled engineer ten minutes.

"Everything's workin' fine, Pam. Why? You playing around with the simulations again?"

"Yes. Just funny you happened to go to the weak point of my last scenario. Plating failure just above and left of Six."

"Coincidence, Pam. You know that."

"Of course I do. Just… odd." She shook off the feeling. "I'm off duty for another half-hour. Let me help out here."

Mal didn't say anything; just tap-slid a holo copy to his right for Pam. All around them the engineering crew continued their preparations, tests, and fine tuning. Their talk soon blended into the rhythmic throb of the fusion engines and left Pam in a comfortable attention of the job at hand.

"Nothing," Mal concluded after ten minutes. "All systems are running fine over the entire shield, including Spike Six."

Pam hesitated. Mal grinned, knowing his friend. When Pam had a notion, she'd pursue it until satisfied. It had kept them alive in the war more than once.

"Fred?" he offered.

"Please. And you explain it, Mal. Fred's a lot better with fact than feeling."

"Gotcha."

Virtually everything about the Horizon was groundbreaking. All ships had—required—gravity plating to control the inertia caused by changes in velocity. But the Horizon had gravity plating in triple redundancy. The best speed recorded to date was 36,000 kps, or twelve percent the speed of light. In just a few hours, the *Horizon* would be doing 12 million kps, or forty times the speed of light. The gravity plating could not fail.

The fusion engines were the best. So, too, the primary cabin of the ship, which maintained habitable conditions for her crew, who would be living inside it for up to three years at a time. The bridge hull was made entirely of an aligned titanium alloy, the hardest, most resistant metal known. It was also capable of becoming transparent.

The crew was handpicked and thoroughly trained, the best in their respective fields, from Captain Tessler all the way to Chef Sam Luther, a master of twenty-eight distinct cooking styles. Nothing was overlooked or compromised. Of all these, however, the ship's ripe, Fred, was the singular example.

Few ships could afford a ship ripe. A unique technology, riping was the reprogramming of a human mind. The only humans allowed to be programmed were those who'd received devastating brain injuries or had been given the death penalty that was about to be carried out. Since riping closed off the original persona and reprogrammed a different section of the ethereal mind, it was a type of death. Thankfully, there were not many "donors".

What Fred had been or done as another person in his original life was not known. Nor if this was his original body. But now he was an insurance policy. In nearly constant access with the secured portion of the puterverse assigned the *Horizon*, Fred saw every aspect of the ship in near instant time. Should the computer core fail, Fred was the only back-up for dozens, perhaps hundreds, of light years. Yet he still maintained a piece of what made him human. This near-perfect blend of human and program meant a final chance of returning home.

"Very well, Commander," Fred replied to Mal's request. "My interface will be in spiral diagnostic for another nineteen minutes and thirty-two seconds, so it is not a problem to meet with Commander Carlson. I will meet her in the forward cargo bay in two minutes precisely."

"Thanks, Fred," Mal acknowledged. "And pay her extra attention, okay? Pam an' I have been together long enough for me to trust her feelings."

"I'll already be giving her my full attention, Commander, so I will not be able to give her extra attention. But I know how entwined your careers are, so I believe I understand your meaning. Fred out."

Fred pulled his forehead away from his puterverse link, breaking hard contact, forcing him to drop from a level 23 access to level 11, which was the safe maximum for humans. By protocol and design, Fred maintained puterverse access at all times.

He slipped his thin body into the transport tube and quickly traveled the eighty meters from his station/quarters in the forward shield to the main hold on the other. Pamela was inspecting the two unpowered 250mm laser cannons.

"Commander Carlson," Fred said once he'd exited and come to attention. "How may I be of service?"

"I wish I knew, Fred," Pam answered honestly. "Commander Stewart apprised you of my concerns?"

"Yes, ma'am. I thank you for letting him explain it. His mental approach is more organized than most and as my primary crew contact, I'm better able to discern his requests. May I ask how I can be of service?"

Pam nodded, hesitant on how to continue. She'd dealt with ripes for years, and Fred for eighteen months, but this was a peculiar situation.

"My thinking is that the incidence of occurrence for the same scenario may not be a fluke but something more purposeful. I want you to see if my thinking is correct, and if so, what the cause is."

"An interesting challenge, Commander," Fred agreed. "While your hunch may be unlikely, I believe it is more likely to have a valid basis."

"You do?" Pam was not really expecting the answer.

"Yes. There are eleven thousand, eight hundred, and thirty-nine possible scenarios available when running the initial light drive program. You have run that program nine hundred and nineteen times since it first went online seven weeks ago, with statistically normal scenarios selection in the first six weeks. The scenario involving the spike hour gravitation flux, however has occurred five times; once in week two and four times in week seven, including your most recent session. To assume it is a coincidence would be foolish."

"All right, then," Pam said. "Pick it apart. And give it high priority, behind only most essential ship needs. We activate the drive in a little over five hours, and I want the answer before then."

"Yes, ma'am." Fred saluted and reentered the transport tube. Before it arrived at the forward shields, he'd already run the scenario two-hundred and five times.

"You wanted to see me, Captain?" Pam stood just outside the door to the Captain's Briefing Room. Taking up the aft portion of the Bridge Deck, the Captain's Quarters had its own gravity controls. It could be set for Martian normal independent of the Bridge. Unfortunately, it was Terran normal to accommodate the dignitaries and media.

"Yes, Carlson." He didn't look up from the tabinal he was reading, but motioned to the chair on his left at the briefing table. "Please…be seated. I know how harsh Terran gravity is. Admittedly, I'm looking to getting back to Martian once we dump…um, safely disembark…our guests after this flight."

Pam gratefully seated herself and patiently awaited his attention. She'd been on bridge duty for ninety minutes and due to the crowd of media and dignitaries coming and going, had been unable to sit. So the offered chair was welcome. In the silence of the next few moments, she contemplated the man she called captain.

Captain William Tessler was a good man and a fine officer. Competent and a stickler for doing things by regulation, he also had some leeway in his thinking and a true concern for his officers and crew. Like Pam, he'd served in the ITA during the Troid Piracy War. Unlike Pam, who'd commanded combat ships, he'd served in Earth defense and not in the asteroid fields. It was whispered throughout the service that the captaincy of the *Horizon* had been given to him rather than Pam because he was Terran. Pam was Martian. Others may have resented it, if true, but it wasn't in Pam's nature; she would gladly serve as his First Officer and felt honored to do so.

Tessler shut off the tabinal and squeezed his eyes firmly for a few seconds.

"There. All caught up reading reports for the next two minutes. And the endless interviews have stopped until after the FTL jump. Speaking of which...Status, please."

"Yes, sir. Ship and crew are fully prepared. The temporary holocam is installed on the bridge and is being tested now."

"Very well. And the *CJ Kelley*?"

"Coming up on us now. She's 2400kps above our current speed and will be alongside in twenty minutes. I'm having her personnel shuttle dock at Deck 5 portside airlock. Sixteen to come aboard. Once the shuttle has returned to her hanger, the *CJ Kelley* will veer back at full speed to a safe distance for our FTL jump, acting as relay for the puterverse uplink."

"Good," Tessler replied, then considered her carefully. "If you're willing, Carlson, I'd like to set rank aside for a moment."

"Yes, sir?"

"I want your honest opinion on our chances of a successful jump. Not the dry numbers, but your gut feeling."

"Sir?"

"I consider myself to be a fully qualified ship's captain. I've been flying for twenty-three years and I've served the Intraplanetary Transit Authority well. I've test-flown a number of prototype ships and been involved with the design and building of many of them. I believe you would have made a fine Captain of the *Horizon*, but I know I am."

"As do I, sir."

Tessler nodded slightly in thanks.

"Before the war, and afterward, you served or commanded slower, older freighters that moved between Luna and Mars. You've done the Jupiter Mail Run multiple times, stopping at countless asteroid mining communities. I've flown to the microcolonies and dwarf planets, too, but always on direct routes, and on ITA vessels that were newer and faster.

"But you've also been in numerous combat missions. The *Tigershark* was a prototype gunship when you took command and flew in extreme conditions for extended periods. I have helped in the making and testing of new ships, but you, Carlson, have put those ships — and other patrol ships well past their prime — into the real. You've been to the place that burns. I have not.

"In short, our careers are similar in length, but very different in content. Now we're going to go together into an entirely new kind of space travel; I as your Captain and you as my First Officer. So I ask again, what do you feel are our chances of a successful FTL jump?"

"We'll be successful, sir."

Tessler waited a moment, then chuckled.

"The typical Martian succinctness. I should have expected that."

"As you know," Pam continued, "Commander Stewart and I have served together ever since I joined my first freighter crew at the age of eight. Sorry…sixteen. He's taught me quite a bit about drives, but it's only the smallest fraction of what he knows. And that's because no matter how much I may learn, Mal *knows* engines and drives in his heart as well as his head. And Mal *knows* that today we'll be travelling faster than light. So I know, too.

"But should we? It's my sense that's what your real question is, Captain. And it's the question that should be asked by everyone. Should we do this? I've always thought of it as going to a first dance as a young tenager — teenager for Earth kids. The discomfort of the formality; the awkwardness of the event; the fear of failure. But mostly, the awareness you're starting a part of your life that you may not be ready for.

"Places that are unreachable now also mean they're a safe distance away. When we generate our singularity in a few hours, that safe zone will instantly be gone. Humankind's dance with whatever — or whomever — is out there will begin. And we can't go back.

"We'll be successful today, I have no doubt. Will we as a race be proud of our accomplishment? Again, I have no doubt. But will we ultimately be glad we did this? Or will we have regrets and think, 'If only we had known'?"

Pam shrugged. "For myself, I'm ready for the first dance."

"Shuttle docking secure, ma'am."

Pam glanced over the airlock readouts automatically and un-necessarily. There were no dummies serving on the *Horizon*.

"Very well, crewman. Begin admitting our guests."

While the sixteen extra dignitaries and media guests — all last-minute add-ons to the maiden voyage trip — boarded and queued for ID verification, Pam stepped over to a nearby comm panel and punched up Fred's comm link.

"I have completed my analysis of both the ship's systems as well as the flight emergency scenarios, Commander," Fred answered without preamble. "Your suspicions are not unfounded."

Pam didn't know whether to feel relieved or worried. Both seem called for.

"Go ahead."

"I ran forensic level diagnostics on the area of the shield as indicated in the scenario involving the failure of the secondary gravity plating near Spike Six. There is no damage, per se. However, there is additional circuitry in that precise location. A search pattern of that circuitry shows no identical nor variant anywhere else on the *Horizon*, the crew, or the guests. It is unique."

"You're sure, Fred?"

"I have eighteen petabytes of data on the ship embedded in my brain, Commander. I am very sure. The circuitry is of a nature and pattern I've never seen before.

"I also have analyzed the scenario itself. I notice you are now with the final group of guests to come aboard before the singularity flight. Tell, me: Is there a Pisces dignitary in that group?"

Pam glanced over at the group of cheerfully talking people. The *homo Marinas* human was easily spotted. His thinner build, washed-out color of his hair, and especially the slightly red streak on his neck, indicating his gills made him stand out even…

The man turned slowly toward Pam and nodded his head in respect, his misty eyes never leaving hers. She instantly recognized him.

"Fred! He's the Pisces from the scenario!"

"I thought that might be the case," Fred replied. "His surface name is Philip Strand. Like the others in this group, he was added unexpectedly within the past five days."

The meaning hit Pam immediately. If he was added only five days ago, how could he have appeared in a scenario that had been programmed months ago? He was involved, clearly, and she needed to isolate and disable him before he could affect whatever…Fred was speaking.

"…not the source of concern, Commander. Quite the opposite; I'm confident he — or rather, the *homo Marinas* people, are the source of the warning. You need to identify a different one of the other fifteen as the saboteur."

"How do you even know there is one?"

"The circuitry I uncovered is incomplete, which is why it escaped notice this entire time. Having the circuitry schematics and knowing its function, I have a reliable estimate of the additional circuitry needed to accomplish that function. You need to determine who has the circuitry and disable the saboteur before it is activated."

"Great," Pam answered. "Very well. Fred, contact security to post outside the both hatches of this Docking Embarkation Room. Two at each door, armed, with orders to immediately disable anyone who comes through without my permission. Then begin scanning everyone in this room for that circuitry. I need you to signal me when I am directly in front of the saboteur."

"Yes, ma'am. I'll hail you on ship-wide comm. Do you have a method of flushing out the saboteur without arousing their suspicions? If that circuitry is activated, we cannot safely generate a singularity."

"I've an idea. Just be ready."

Pam turned off the comm and walked directly to Philip Strand, who seemed to be expecting it. She hoped he would catch on to her attempt to use him as a distraction.

When one meter away, Pam suddenly stood at attention, then snapped a bow deep at the waist to Strand. She then turned her back and held her hands palms up away from her sides.

"My life is yours, Philip Strand." She remained in that position until she felt his firm hand on her shoulder, whereupon she turned around.

"The honor of your life preserves it, Commander Pamela Carlson, of the Tabor home." Strand flowed into a bow that was possible only by a Pisces. "Your greeting honors my family and my race." He rose from his bow.

Pam looked beyond him and addressed the others. No need to call attention; everyone was watching.

"Most of you probably do not know this gentleman. His name is Philip Strand and he is the Chief Magistrate of Atlantis, the Pisces home city. I am bound by protocol to introduce him to each of you individually. It is also my honor to do so. This level of Pisces greeting is very straightforward. Simply speak your name while looking the Chief Magistrate directly in the eye. Then bow, but make no contact."

Pam allowed Strand to go first, indicating his trust in her. He stepped to the first guest, a middle-aged man of Hispanic descent and with a slight paunch. The man stood straight and looked Strand directly in the eyes.

"I am Miguel Santos-Rodriguez, ambassador for King Fidel IV and representing the Cuban Kingdom." He gave a sharp handsome bow, which Strand returned with a flowing bow.

They stepped up to the second, a silver-haired woman with Scandinavian features. Name, title, and bow were repeated and returned.

Slowly they worked their way down the line. There was no impatience and the formality and respect was quite real. Pam didn't have the heart to tell them that there was no Chief Magistrate of Atlantis and that Philip Strand was probably little more than a minor diplomat, if even that.

They'd just finished with the ninth guest, a man with a beard and a definite military bearing, ready to step to the tenth guest, when the ship's comm sounded a whistle.

"Commander Carlson, please report to Captain Tessler at once. Commander Carlson, please report to Captain Tessler."

Instantly, Pam shot her fist up and punched the man directly in the throat with all her strength, hoping to break his neck. He jerked his head back at the last instant, but nonetheless instinctively grasped his neck with both hands. Pam started to kick at his left knee to shatter it and further incapacitate him when she was shoved back. Not by the saboteur but by Strand.

Strand was incredibly strong, a trait in all members of the genetically engineered *homo Marinas* race. With no difficulty, he seized the man's wrists and slammed them back against the bulkhead. He moved his face to within centimeters of the saboteur's face and stared into his eyes.

"Death has arrived," he concluded quietly. "There is no light of hope in your eyes, nor the comfort of dark. Only the mud of hatred; the unbreathable fear of the unknown that silences your children. For that I and my children will grieve."

Strand released his wrists and stepped back. As he did, he slipped his right hand across the man's throat. There was a flicker of a steel finger blade, and then blood gushed from the wound. He sank to the floor, dead.

Pam stepped up and looked down at the man, blood still pooling. All were in stunned shock.

Earth date: Monday, September 22, 2245 AD 3:26pm (UTC)
Martian date: Tujun 19, 104 MD
100 Astronomical Units from Earth

"Subspace field construction is complete and stable." Chief Engineer Mahlon Stewart said clearly. Pam cocked her head slightly and turned toward Mal at his bridge station. There seemed to be an undertone of annoyance. Mal wanted to be in Engineering and not on the overcrowded Bridge. "Fusion engines at full, running point zero five one light speed."

"Acknowledged, Chief. Prime singularity feed for mass insertion into the subspace matrix," Captain Tessler replied calmly. He turned to his left, toward Pam. "Ship's status, if you please, First."

She glanced at her station holopanels even though she had just done so.

"We're in the black, Captain," she said crisply. "All departments on continuous reporting. No alerts; no cautions."

"Priming singularity feed," Mal reported. "Light speed available in ten seconds."

"Thank you, Engineer. Helm, Bridge hull to transparent."

A slight hum of power through the hull's aligned titanium and suddenly the entirety of space was viewable, cut off only by the massive bulk of the forward shield. Pam glanced at Spike Six, but made no comment.

"Singularity feed primed; subspace matrix ready in all respects," Mal announced. "Light speed available at your command, Captain."

Captain Tessler paused. He glanced around the bridge, filled with guests and dignitaries, all of them stunned into silence. Even the *homo Marinas* people had a representative. Directly in front, between him and the Pilot/Navigator stations, was a huge holocam, broadcasting the historic event to Earth.

"First Officer, please mark the time."

"September 22, 2245; 3:26pm, Coordinated Universal Time."

"Engage singularity drive," Tessler ordered.

"Aye, sir," Mal replied. "We're chasing the ball."

There was no surge of acceleration. Instead, the heavy throb of the fusion engine dropped and was replaced by a rumble deep inside the belly of the *Horizon* as the singularity drive activated.

A collective gasp went up as the stars went from pinpoints of unmoving light to bright lines of white. There was a flash from forward of the bows that spilled over the shield edges and cascaded toward them like an ocean of the bluest water. It was no sooner seen than it was gone, falling behind the *Horizon* and taking the stars with it.

"Helm. Speed," Captain Tessler requested.

"Eleven point two light speed and accelerating," Ensign Behrens answered.

Pam smiled, her heart racing as fast as the ship.

"People, we just stepped onto the ballroom floor. Let's not trip on our petticoats."

THE JANUS CHOICE

Jeff Young

"MAKE A HOLE!"

Danvers heard as he was pushed out of the way by a medical tech leading a stretcher team up the ramp to the transition index. He caught a brief glimpse of the body they were carrying and recognized his superior's black-striped tunic. Angry red burns, seeping yellow fluid covered Brandiwicz's face. The arriving team of envoys scattered to either side of the platform to let the medical crew pass. Danvers saw the medic's forms elongate as they entered the index's wavering line and disappear from view.

"You Danvers?" asked a woman as she moved down the ramp, her eyes following the second wave team as they offloaded additional supplies.

Still in shock, he nodded once. Upon further inspection, he decided she had the look of a traveler, skin worn down by the suns of other worlds, hair bleached and brittle from odd radiations. The tag on her blue pullover with red stripes said CERDAIN. He wracked his brain trying to connect the name to any details concerning new arrivals.

"Well, how long will it take you to get me to Brandiwicz? I'm not exactly blessed with a lot of time," she asked.

He took a breath and said as evenly as he could manage, "Ma'am, they just took him out on a stretcher. His condition did not look good."

"Huh," she sighed, turning about to look at the transition point. "Well that turns this whole situation to recycle." Her head snapped back to him. "You're his assistant, right?" She barely gave him a chance to nod in confirmation before continuing, "Well I hope you're up to it, because we need to find out why the Kamanti have suddenly decided we need to leave their world. That transition index will be open for just 24 more hours. The next one isn't scheduled until next month."

"Brandiwicz never had any trouble with the natives before." Danvers shut the gate behind him as he ushered the woman forward. "You're not implying that one of them attacked him, are you?"

"I have no idea. The one person I needed to speak with just went where I can't reach him." She shrugged. "As for a Kamanti harming Brandiwicz, our behavioral model has issues," she added swinging up into the passenger seat of the skim. Cerdain leaned forward eyeing the spidering cracks in the windscreen. "We wouldn't be on the verge of packing up the entire setup and leaving if he were here to give us some idea of what's happened. This has turned into a colossal fiasco that keeps getting worse."

Taking a moment to choke back the less-than- respectful replies that came to mind, Danvers managed, "It's easy to look at this in a certain way when you are part of the second wave. We've achieved something here with the Kamanti that's been the envy of other first contact teams. Now, with no warning, everything we've put together is going to just vanish. We were notified right before your arrival. As Brandiwicz's assistant I'll do everything I can to figure out how he was injured and if it is related to this situation." He threw the skim into gear without so much as a glance at her.

Danvers felt her glaring at him and ignored it, pushing the skim out of the rear exit of the embassy compound onto the flat plains and their dark red grasses. The greenish sky was full of pollen clouds and the winking jewels of the enigmatic light sail farms.

Humanity was struggling to understand the machines, making them a prime source of interest to the contact team's scientists. The power they generated was distributed across the planet by what the researchers believed were wormhole threads. Since it took a massive amount of power to generate transition indexes, the only kind of wormholes humanity knew how to make; there was a definite focus on understanding how the energy was transferred from the solar farms to the city below using a minute amount of energy to initiate the threads.

With a wide arc, Danvers brought them around the exterior of the Diplomatic Compound to the edge of the urban sprawl that surrounded the Kamanti city of Tuanach. Maybe it said something about humanity that they were placed beyond the outskirts of the city and, for the most part, forgotten. Danvers liked to assume it was an honor. He put the errant thought out his head and guided the skim into Tuanach. The wide streets of the city gave him plenty of room to maneuver, and he focused on his driving instead of his passenger's ire.

The outpost's director, Weavir, was still trying to find a way back into the good graces of the loose association of Kamanti leaders. Danvers wished him luck. For eight weeks, Danvers had enjoyed the pleasures of this world and its unusual people. It looked as though that time was about to come to an abrupt end. Center had punched the transition index through and gave the envoys three months to determine if it was worth the energy cost of making it a permanent settlement.

Now that Cerdain was here, she acted as if she were going to single-handedly clean up the situation. "Where are we going, Danvers?" she asked, her annoyance clear. "The information I need is back in the compound. Now is not the time for a tour of the city."

"You will want to see where Brandiwicz worked. There could be something in his quarters that will offer more insight into the situation."

"Look, Danvers, why don't you make things clear for me? I talked to Weavir before I got here. I talked to everyone. I even talked to that damned archaeologist, Pergman, who did nothing but complain since the natives have a taboo against digging up the past and he can't do his job. I still can't get a clear answer. Why are we being asked to leave?"

Since they had almost arrived at the set of rooms Brandiwicz was given by the Kamanti, Danvers considered his reply and drove on in silence. After he'd pulled the skim to one side of a low building, he turned to her. "The most difficult part of the situation, ma'am, is that we're not being told to leave. Instead we've been told we can't stay. It is an odd conundrum. Weavir says that he gets the feeling that the Kamanti are acting as if they don't want us involved in something. It's frustrating everyone who's been working here. And Pergman, he's just annoying and has a problem with authority."

Cerdain slid out of the skim, her footfalls kicking up the city's ever-present yellow dust. She stood for a moment looking at him across the hood, her arms crossed over her chest. "I know plenty about disappointment, Danvers. Being relegated to clean up someone else's mess is never going to sit well with me."

Danvers turned away as quickly as possible, trying to wipe the scowl off of his face. Who the hell was she, charging in here as if she really knew what was going on? He wanted to turn back and argue with

Cerdain, but instead he clenched his hands into fists and led her down a small walk between the rounded walls of the low buildings. He could almost feel the frustration radiating off her. It made him quicken his pace.

The exterior of the building was worn down, like everything in Tuanach. Time lay heavily on the Kamanti. The owner of the sprawling building that housed Brandiwicz's rooms waited for them at the elliptical gate. Danvers was always struck by the fact that the Kamanti were symmetrical in body plan, but radially rather than bilaterally.

Their bodies consisted of eight appendages grouped into four legs that led up to a cylindrical waist. The Kamanti arms were arrayed in a square around a central gullet. Like everyone, Danvers got past the desire to look for eyes and stopped trying to categorize them into genders since they reproduced through budding. The skin of the Kamanti not only acted as a receptor of light, but also generated it. Like the environs, their skins at rest were dusky yellow broken up by stripes of dark red.

Light rippled across the Kamanti as it walked toward them, photophores in its flesh firing in sequence. Danvers tipped his tablet fleck at the Kamanti and it began translating, "For now, you are welcome, associate of Brandiwicz."

Cerdain was already stepping forward, when Danvers slid sideways to cut her off. Holding the small tablet in front of him, he said with respect to the Kamanti, "Last Light of Day, we are happy to find you here. We must look at Brandiwicz's rooms. Will you let us in?"

It watched the play of colors across the surface of Danvers's computing fleck and replied in kind. "Perhaps you can start to put Brandiwicz's effects in order?"

As Danvers suspected, Cerdain wasn't about to let that pass without a response. Her fleck flashed back at the native, "Is that a request or a demand?"

Turning on its hinged legs, the Kamanti fired back a single flash of light. Danvers turned away, hiding a grin. He was certain that "yes" was not the answer that Cerdain was expecting. He leaned over, tugging at the latch on the front door to slide it open and asked, "Coming, ma'am?"

She responded by impatiently gesturing him onward.

Stepping inside, Danvers was reminded of the tremendous flex-ibility of the Kamanti, since the turns from room to room were sharp and abrupt without angles. As he led Cerdain further into the dwelling, they passed a small kitchen, a cot under a rounded window, and an open garden. At last they came into a larger area where a desk sat against the curved wall. Cerdain began to shuffle through the material on the top of the desk.

Stepping into the final room, Danvers took a moment to splash water from a low basin onto his face and run his fingers through his close-cropped reddish hair. He looked up at the dingy flex mirror Brandiwicz had tacked to the wall and held back a sigh. His reflection was filled with tired resignation. He frowned and stepped closer as he noticed something written on the surface of the mirror. Danvers could just make out the words, "Being here doesn't mean you belong." It was a rather depressing thought, backed up by the reality of the current situation. Respect for Brandiwicz outweighed Danvers guilt as he reached up and wiped away the comment. Cerdain was calling him when he turned back toward the office.

"What do you make of this, Danvers?" She was looking at her fleck with a curious expression. Danvers glanced over her shoulder. The image on the fleck wavered for a moment before a Kamanti came into focus. The viewpoint pulled back until the native could be easily seen. The mirrored surface of one of the many water retention ponds reflected back the Kamanti's image. It stood, rocking back and forth, focused on the view before it. Brandiwicz's voice broke into the recording, "The Kamanti are susceptible to these fits of interior retrospection. It is almost as if they have a problem with being themselves. This along with other evidence, such as the ingrained aversion to examine collective past, illustrates how far we are from understanding our hosts."

"So he knew he was failing? Why wouldn't he ask for help?" Cerdain asked flipping the fleck back and forth.

"I wouldn't say he was failing. I think that everyone assumed that the Kamanti would be easy to understand since a great deal of their life and culture appears simplistic. But they are aliens and vastly different from us in some ways. Take for example how the Kamanti learn. The Kamanti have something similar to our mirror neurons. The first time you watch someone do a task, a series of neurons will fire, even though you are not the one doing the task. When you later accomplish the task yourself, this same arc of neurons will fire again.

The Kamanti have them in droves. We think they educate their young while they are still sessile by imprinting them with layers of visual information that gets absorbed and then acted upon using these mirror neurons. That's like programming their young. It's only once the young become motile that they actually begin to actively use the information to make choices. This alone makes their culture and their reactions very different from those of humanity."

"If that's the case, then Brandiwicz would have figured that into the overall cultural image of the Kamanti. So what did he miss?" Not waiting for his answer, Cerdain continued to flip through the fleck chits layered on the top of Brandiwicz's desk. "What do you think Brandiwicz did to himself, Danvers? The report I read on the way over here said he never regained consciousness before they shipped him out. What can you tell me about his state of mind before his injury?"

"I think sometimes he got frustrated by situations beyond his control. He would have what looked like the answer and it would turn out to be an inexplicable aspect of the Kamanti behavior that had not been fully observed."

"Yet, you still defend his competency." She sat the fleck down on the desktop for a moment to look at him.

"Up until a day ago, we were very successful here. That success came from the groundwork that Brandiwicz laid. Just because the man had an accident doesn't mean that he is responsible if the mission fails."

Cerdain's fleck chimed. With a faraway look, she considered the message, but the moment did not last. "Gather up all the loose chits, we've got another problem to consider."

He slid his arm across the table scooping up the remaining info chits before dropping them into his thigh pocket. Then Danvers waved her toward the door. After passing by, Cerdain told him over her shoulder, "Brandiwicz is dead. If he didn't injure himself, we're looking at a murder."

Coming to a halt in the doorway, Danvers slumped against the rounded frame. His eyes weren't focusing and the dusty yellow of Tuanach faded to a blur. His mentor, colleague and friend was dead. Right now the last person he wanted to hear that from was walking away. He was briefly tempted to slip out the back into Tuanach's winding alleys. Cerdain would never find him. But the chance that she might find out why Brandiwicz had perished was one of the few things that made him straighten up, pull his tunic straight and lope after her.

She continued, "If that wasn't bad enough, Pergman has also gone missing. He sent his empty skim back on autopilot. Your staff is annoyed. We've been asked to retrieve him since we're closest." Danvers opened his mouth to tell her about Pergman's personal tracking tag but Cerdain cut him off, "And just in case you weren't certain, that annoys *me*." She headed toward the entrance, not waiting for Danvers to show her out.

At the doorway, Danvers stopped and looked back. He was still in shock over Brandiwicz's death, but something unexpected caught his attention. By the entrance was a little alcove. It was usually empty, but there was something in it. He stepped closer and reached in to pull out a strange, brown object. It was about the size of his thumb, hollow and covered in unusual rectangular markings, sealed at one end. The other terminus was a jagged edge. It was the design on the outside that had caught his attention. Kamanti artwork was full of spirals, not squares. What was he looking at? Perplexed, Danvers took it with him.

Cerdain was already in the driver's seat, tapping her fingers on the dash. "Get in. Collecting missing team members was never part of my plan. Who knows what the hell happened to Pergman"

Danvers leaned back as the skim shot forward. "He's not in danger. The Kamanti are not a violent species."

"Not violent? Look, just because they are not actively seeking to hurt you doesn't mean that they won't step out of the way and let you take the hit."

"Ma'am, I can't say that I agree with most of your views." He paused to look down at his fleck, then pointed to the right, "Wait, take a right here." He looked at his fleck again. "According to the locator on Pergman, he's way out in the foothills past the edge of the plains."

The skim picked up speed, its aircushion protecting them from the uneven portions of the terrain. Looking over at Cerdain as she pushed the skim faster and faster, Danvers broached the question that gnawed at him. "Ma'am, is there a particular reason you happen to be unhappy with Pergman and Brandiwicz?"

She gave him a sharp glance and drove on, remaining silent. The awkward moment continued.

"If you must know, Danvers...we are having a great deal of trouble with the Kamanti cultural modeling program we are running. I can only assume that our two most direct sources of information must be flawed, hence my displeasure. We cannot nail down the correct behavior model for the Kamanti." She took a breath. "Therefore, we can't come up with their reasons behind this sudden about face. With the data we've received so far, I've been given a month to get this running properly. In case it has escaped you, I don't consider failure an option. Our part of this expedition was to be next. Since receiving word of the Kamanti's desire for us to vacate, Center has given the whole embassy two days to finish its mission. At that point, the transition index will open and Weavir needs to be ready to give them a yea or nay."

"So I take it that the cultural modeling is your project?"

"If you must ask, it's unlikely you'll ever be called perceptive." Cerdain shook her head and turned her attention back to driving, shutting him out completely.

Watching the buildings diminish as the skim lifted out onto the plain, Danvers looked back at Tuanach. *There is still so much to learn from the Kamanti,* he mused. Their natural command over light gave them a unique perspective on such subjects as luminous data storage and light propulsion. Never mind that the natives were close-mouthed about their biology and even more reticent to talk about their past. This amazing world with its casual mix of technology and massive communal living was a rich treasure trove of knowledge.

A mile-long plume of yellow dust trailed after the skim as the heat from the plains rose in shimmering waves. Danvers spared a glance at Cerdain. Wisps of lighter hair fanned out around her head and danced about in the wind. Her blue and red striped embassy pullover was already bunched and rucked. Her clenched grasp on the steering column made the tendons in her hands stand up like cords. She was focused all right and that was what worried him. Cerdain was so focused she might miss potential solutions.

Glancing at her fleck, Cerdain adjusted their course away from the light farms overhead and said, "I don't have to worry about driving us through one of the wormhole threads transmitting power do I?"

"There's no physical connection between the light sail farm and the receivers in the city, it's just not possible." Danvers realized his tone was a bit sharp and added, "So much of the Kamanti technology is passive in nature. The truth is, I'm jealous of them. It doesn't break down, so they don't worry about it. As a civilization, they've reached a point where infrastructure is no longer an issue." For a moment, he considered her. It was an odd question, surely she knew — then he had it. She was probing him, deciding how much he knew about the wormhole threads.

The tension drained out of Cerdain. "Don't get me wrong, Danvers. I want this to work. It has to work. Don't ever think that I'm not impressed by what I've seen in my short time here. But keep in mind; I've been building a cultural model that will give future expeditions an immediate head start on understanding the Kamanti. Which, if things do not change, will be useless."

Danvers looked away. Her abrasive nature had resurfaced again. *A very short moment of calm in a perpetual storm*, he thought.

The skim approached the hills now as they headed into canyon country. Soon, Cerdain had to bank back and forth as they entered the maze of arroyos. She forced the skim higher on its aircushion as Danvers checked his fleck. They were about two kilometers from Pergman. What worried him was the lack of signal from the archaeologist's skim. Pergman couldn't have walked all the way out here.

"Down here," Cerdain motioned, turning the skim 180 degrees to plunge into a tight gully. Light filtered down through the reddish walls of stone, giving everything a ruddy cast. The skim came to an abrupt halt, throwing Danvers toward the windscreen. Pushing himself back, he resisted the urge to snap.

The arroyo narrowed to a winding path, and Cerdain brought them to a halt in the last possible flat space. Fleck held in front of her, she was already out of the skim and heading over to the left. Light from the display's surface playing over her features had Danvers imagining what she might look like in conversation with the Kamanti and he almost smiled. He pulled himself out, silently berated himself, and found his footing on the rough ground, ready to follow her between the looming walls of the canyon. Colored bands crawled through the twisting columns of rock formed by the very wind borne sands that annoyed his eyes now.

"Only a damn archaeologist would enjoy coming here," Cerdain called over her shoulder.

"Or a geologist."

"Don't feel you need to argue with me on principal, Danvers."

Another smile crossed his lips. Turning one final corner, they found their way blocked by a mound of scree and rubble. "Well that's new," remarked Danvers as he dropped to one knee to gather up a handful of the ocher dirt, sifting it through his fingers.

"Looks like your archaeologist hasn't been ignoring restrictions."

"Pergman. Well, he was never very good at following orders to the letter."

"Now you're wondering if this is the reason behind our sudden need to leave the planet," Cerdain said dryly, "You're not the only one. Any wonder why Weavir felt it necessary to hit him with a tracking tag..." She'd reached the top of the rock fall and stopped with her hands on her hips. "Get up here, you won't believe this."

As Danvers pulled himself up, he realized they were on the edge of a large, bowl-shaped excavation. But that was the rim, at its center a tunnel descended out of sight. "Weavir's going to have Pergman's head."

"He can get in line. I'm here first," was Cerdain's waspish reply. Already she'd stalked over to the guide rope running from the rim to the tunnel and began to make her way down.

Danvers followed. He had little choice. A string of tiny, blue-white lights descended into the depths along the ceiling of the tunnel. Together they went downward.

Their descent was rapid, once he got used to Cerdain randomly tugging on the line below him. There was something here he was missing...Danvers stopped, looking closely at the patterning on the wall of the tunnel. There were spiraling grooves the whole way down. Almost as if— "Bastard," he snapped, slapping the wall.

"Figured it out?" asked Cerdain moving onward, "Pergman ought to hope I just seal up this tunnel and forget about it. Unlicensed and unapproved use of nano-dissociators, whatever career he had—it's over. I hope the natives don't exercise any of their territorial rights."

Increasing the speed of his descent, Danvers slid along the scree trying to catch up. In fact, he was moving so quickly that when the tunnel's pitch leveled out, he fell forward. Cerdain reached down and caught his hand hauling him to his feet. Danvers was struck by her silence and the intensity of her stare. Following her gaze, he saw the first of the immense cylinders.

They were a dark, coppery red. The glow from brighter lights stuck to the ceiling fell onto three of the objects. Danvers walked up to the closest and reached out a hand. He caught himself before touching the cylinder, mesmerized by its strange, indistinct nature. Call it a hunch, but there was something about the patina that made him pull out his fleck and do a quick scan. Viewed with a higher magnification, it became obvious that the exterior of the cylinder was made up of an immense number of tiny hook-like cilia, all of which were canted upward. Upon further inspection Danvers saw the cilia moved in a spiral pattern almost too slowly to be seen.

"Don't..." he warned and then stopped, realizing that Cerdain was now looking over his shoulder at the fleck's image instead of reaching out as he had.

"Can't imagine what touching that would do, but I'm not going to give it a try. Consider this for a second. If you were to bury that cylinder in the ground; wouldn't the cilia propel it back up to the surface?"

Stepping around the circumference, Danvers looked down at yet another hole. Pergman had been quite busy. He wondered how far below the cylinders' origins lay. And the real reason behind all of this was? Something else caught his eye. Rectangular shapes were embossed on the cylinder's exterior. One had to account for the cylinder's size and the bad lighting, but the shapes were familiar. He pulled out the small cylinder he found in Brandiwicz's rooms. He started to call out to Cerdain, but noticed a shadow moving across the light at the far end of the tunnel.

Cerdain was already moving forward. "Pergman! What the hell is going on here?"

Circling around the cylinder, Danvers put on a burst of speed trying to intercept her before the encounter turned violent.

The archaeologist stopped in mid-stride, a stunned look on his face. His long hair was pulled back in clumps of dreadlocks and the single suit he wore was streaked with multicolored dust. A series of programmable plastic tables were arranged in an arc behind him. Various implements and specimen bins were scattered on top of them. In the middle lay a very familiar rod-like shape — that mirrored the one in Danvers's pocket.

"Did Weavir send you? I'm not quite ready yet. There's so much more to find here. We've got to take the time and pack things up properly."

"Properly?" Tension and anger marred Cerdain's features as she marched forward, hands clenched at her sides. "Tell me why the unauthorized use of nano-dissociators, excavation against the express permission of the natives, and the use of embassy property to accomplish your personal agenda would have anything in common with doing this in a proper fashion?"

"Wait," interrupted Danvers, "you're saying that Weavir is aware of what you're doing here?"

"Certainly," Pergman said, indignation wrinkling up his features, "and I also gave all of my findings to Brandiwicz."

Sharing a brief look with Cerdain, Danvers took a breath before continuing. "Well, I think maybe our anger may be a bit misdirected. Pergman, just what is going on here?"

Pergman took several steps back and pulled a sling chair out from behind the worktables. He slid back into it and proceeded to stare at the two intruders. Leaning forward, he spread his hands and said, "What we don't know about this culture is staggering. Even now, I've made some finds that I can barely explain. There are elements at work here that run beneath the veneer of Kamanti society. But before I could really start digging into things Brandiwicz stepped in. Weavir will hold him responsible."

"He's dead," snapped Cerdain, "So that's hardly relevant."

Pergman sat stunned for a moment, his mouth open. But he was quick with the rejoinder, "Who the hell are you?"

"This is Cerdain, she is with the second wave team and in charge of the Kamanti behavioral model," Danvers said. Then he asked, "Just what did you find?"

"I found the one thing that was hidden right in front of us all along — evidence of a second race...the Mahanti.

"When I look at the Kamanti, I see a culture that has worn down so many of its distinguishing marks, that it reminds me of a river pebble. You can keep trying to get a grasp on it, but it slips away every time. There are plenty aspects of the Kamanti that just don't add up. But they've been around so long that they've tinkered with their biology and psychology. But the basics of their makeup, now that's where things get interesting."

"Academics," Cerdain shook her head in disgust. "Can you get to the point?"

Danvers intervened. "Start with something simple. What are the cylinders?"

Pergman shook his head, he started to answer but stopped unsure of what to reveal. Steepling his hands in front of his face, he said quietly, "Those are the arks that hold the Mahanti culture. At least this set is, the deep resonance wave scans show another set even further down. After that there's another and another. It's like there are waves of them launched from some set of machines deep down in the mantle. They are all over this world, slowly digging their way up. I had to dig down 15 miles just to get these." The archaeologist got to his feet, walking over to stand in front of the closest cylinder. "This," he said, motioning toward the towering object, "just screams time capsule to me. Look, the Kamanti didn't want us prying into their history, because they've been culturally programmed not to. They didn't want us investigating their biology because it might reveal things out about their nature." Now, Pergman stopped and looked at Cerdain, studying her face. The mask of indifference she'd put on slipped for a moment.

Pointing a finger at her, he said, "You knew. You knew about their biology. I wonder where that information came from."

She looked down, unwilling to meet either of their gazes. "I had to, in order to properly flesh out the cultural model."

"So just where did you get this information from?" demanded Danvers, beginning to feel his own ire rising. All of the double-dealing and maneuvering finally pushed him to the breaking point.

"It was gathered surreptitiously, of course. Samples were taken here and there. Discrete probes were sent out," replied Cerdain

"More nanotech right?" Danvers asked with a touch of anger.

"Of course. But you see, Danvers, what we discovered didn't help us answer any of our questions. We found out that the Kamanti had rebuilt their biology."

"Ok, so that's something new to me, but what does it have to do with the Mahanti? What were they?"

Cerdain looked to Pergman for the answer. He was walking behind a cylinder tapping his lip. When he reappeared, he said, "The Mahanti and Kamanti were co-extant species, both of which could have developed into the natural owners of this world. Their biology was very similar, both radially symmetric, both photophore bearing, and both exceptional in terms of intelligence. If you look at the basements of the buildings of Tuanach, you'll find there are foundations upon foundations upon foundations. The city is built up like a nautilus shell. Go far enough and there's a point where the architecture changes to something more angular in nature, at that point you're looking at the Mahanti's work." The archaeologist's hand hovered over the cylinder in admiration. "When I looked at resonance photos of deeply buried cities, I found spiraling architecture down so far and then the rest was all angular. Go on down and you find more spirals once again. At some point the cultures realized that one of them would become dominant and supersede the other. Humanity didn't share Earth with the Neanderthals and these two cultures realized they couldn't either."

"So the Kamanti were the winners, and now they have a collective cultural guilt because of it. Then we come along and discover the truth by breaking a taboo that requires us to leave. Have I got it?" Cerdain summarized.

Danvers stepped closer to the specimen tables as an argument commenced. He reached down and picked up a small, hollow cylinder. It was no surprise that it matched the one from his pocket. The same angular designs covered its exterior. Interestingly enough, they were laid out in a spiral pattern. Here it was, the two aspects of the civilizations mated together. An idea began to form. Pieces were sliding together in the larger framework of the puzzle.

Danvers cleared his throat. Pergman and Cerdain both paused to look at him. Holding up the two halves of the cylindrical container, Danvers asked, "Just what was in this?"

Pergman looked at it for a second and then answered, "There was a dull, translucent rod decorated with more of the same inscription. One of these is at the center of every one of the time capsules."

"Can I guess that you gave the rod to Brandiwicz?"

"Yes, he asked specifically for it when I showed him the inventory. Wait, what are you implying?"

"Not yet, please," Danvers said and then turned to Cerdain. "If you had to guess, just how extensively have the Kamanti modified themselves?"

"Quite a bit. It's almost as if they decided to refine their life processes and do away with any evolutionary dead ends. Since I've just heard about the Mahanti, I can't make any comparisons. So, if you're asking did they try to blend the species, I can't say."

"I don't think it was that simple," Danvers answered. "I think we made a lot of assumptions when we tried to find out what happened here. We looked at things on our timescale. We look at how humans would make any given decision, clouding our findings." He looked at the cylinder again. "Maybe you were right, Pergman, but it's not a time capsule...more like a recipe." Danvers took a breath and then asked, "How long would it take one of these cylinders to reach the surface?"

Pergman scratched at his chin. "I don't know. A quarter of a million years? Longer? You're saying that they were seeded at that depth so they would reappear on the surface at some point in the future?"

"I think that makes sense," was Cerdain's reply, "But look we have more information now. We should get that to Weavir. There is even the possibility that we can use what we know to convince the Kamanti to let us stay."

Danvers looked about the confined area. There didn't seem to be a reason to stay anymore. "I vote to leave."

"Fine," Pergman replied and then took a brief tour around the area, shutting down anything that was still running. He reached into a carry sack and pulled out a small winch motor. "This will make it easier for us to get out."

"For you maybe, but what about us?" asked Cerdain.

"Oh, I'll just lower it down the hole again."

"In that case, I'll go first," she said grabbing the small motor from the archaeologist. Within seconds she'd vanished from sight. The winch slid down the cable after a little while and Pergman was the next to ascend.

Danvers was surprised when the machine arrived for him. Both Cerdain and Pergman had something to hide. He hesitated, looking around. Even though he'd suggested leaving, there were still a great many unanswered questions here. Then he started to work his way up the tunnel.

Brandiwicz would have understood. The message on his mirror said it all. The divide between the thought processes of the Kamanti/Mahanti and humanity couldn't be breached. It could only be approximated. The solution that the two races had created was simply too alien.

Danvers reached up and grasped Pergman's offered hand when he reached the edge of the excavation. Swinging back, he looked down. The hole was almost as full of secrets as the people he worked with and that brought him up short — the kind of secrets one would kill for? Cerdain and Pergman stared at him as he turned away from the dig site. He threw himself into the back seat, Cerdain took the driver's seat and the archeologist slid in beside her. It was a long, quiet ride back to the compound.

When they reached the edge of Tuanach, Danvers recognized a very familiar figure just off the edge of the road to the Diplomatic Compound. He tapped Cerdain on the shoulder. "I'll walk from here." She looked at him sharply, but brought the skim to a halt. As they drove away, Danvers saw their heads lean together; just how many of the details of their conspiracy would be hatched after he left? He turned back to the Kamanti edging forward out of the shadows.

He looked at the patterns on the Kamanti's skin. What was Last Light of Day doing here? Before he could bring his fleck up to ask the question, the Kamanti lit up with a rush of color.

"Why are you here?" it asked.

Danvers hesitated, every time he spoke to a Kamanti, it always felt like there was an extra level of depth to their conversation. Even now he wasn't certain that the question was directed at him or at humanity as a whole. Perhaps it was best to limit the potential for error. "The others left me behind." Realizing he might not get the opportunity again, he transmitted to the fleck a question, "Last Light of Day did Brandiwicz ever show you something, something important?"

The native didn't answer him; instead it shuffled around him and took a few steps down the roadway back toward Tuanach. When it turned back, Last Light of Day leaned toward Danvers, a human affectation that Brandiwicz had taught them, to indicate to whom they were speaking. His fleck translated, "He showed me the future and the past all in one flash."

Danvers approached the Kamanti. "He showed you a rod and that rod flashed you with a burst of information."

"No," replied Last Light of Day, "The light I saw was of other ideas. Ideas I can't forget—ideas that are not part of what it means to be Kamanti." The Kamanti's light swirled. "Danvers, I glow with these ideas. Others look at me and they see the ideas and then they are part of them as well. I went into the crèche as I always do. I shared with the young. But I couldn't share the things they needed to know. No, I shared with them this infestation that is changing me. I look at myself and I am not me! Danvers, what did he do to us?"

Stepping backward, Danvers covered his eyes. It must have seemed like the perfect solution at the time. Bury the capsules; but allow them to return after ages of the Kamanti civilization so it could be the Mahanti's turn. Beyond them further still was another fleet of capsules digging their way up to recreate the Kamanti once more. How long had the cycle gone on? Yet no one counted on some external force with more curiosity than common sense. Had Brandiwicz even realized what he'd done?

Could one write memes in luminous information? The Kamanti would take it in with no buffers since that was the way they were taught during childhood. All that had to be added was a compulsion to share and there was a self-propagating reiteration of an entire culture.

The Kamanti were right, humanity did not belong here. Humanity had started the process prematurely in ignorance. That same ignorance could infect the nascent society that was forming and corrupt everything, every being.

Dropping his hands, he forced open his eyes. With the fleck, he spoke heavy with regret, "I would like to believe Brandiwicz made a mistake. He did show you your future, a future decided upon by your distant ancestors. But this was not meant to happen for many more years. I think he made a mistake, intending no harm." He paused trying to come up with more, wondering if Brandiwicz had done this intentionally trying to discover the technology behind the wormhole threads hidden in the cultural download. The Kamanti, however, wanted to have the last word.

"You do not have to go, but you cannot stay. Tuanach is not safe for you." With that enigmatic comment, it turned and walked slowly into the city.

Danvers watched the small form grow indistinct. As he turned back, he faced the high wall of the Diplomatic Compound and began his own walk. When he neared the gate, Danvers became aware of movement overhead. Typically, they were so high up it was easy to ignore them, but the light sail farms had clustered together. Their white indistinct forms were moving into an eye-blearing sheet. Danvers could not say what type of survival instinct made him begin to run, but he threw himself through the gate. Turning quickly, he shut the heavy door and rolled into the shadow of the curving wall.

There was an incandescent flash that bounced from every surface of the Compound above him. The silence that followed was profound, finally broken by a loud hiss, like a rising wind began. When the pressure wave struck, the Compound rang like a giant bell and the omnipresent yellow dust flew over everything like a cyclone.

When they found him, Danvers was still huddled against the wall. The others from the Diplomatic team pulled him to his feet and slung his arms over their shoulders. Together they stumbled into the Compound. When they reached the second floor, Danvers caught a glimpse of the sheet of molten magma that once was Tuanach. The light sail farms must have passed several of the mouths of the wormhole threads over the city reducing it to a glowing ember. Just like everything else the Kamanti and Mahanti had built, even the premature launch of a civilization had a fail-safe built into it. That defined their technology to a point—it just worked.

Eventually, Cerdain collected every one of the chits from Danvers. He handed them over with no resistance. Maybe one of them contained the secret they were seeking—the creation and control of wormhole threads. After all, they'd just survived a demonstration of how powerful a weapon they could be. She left him the small hollowed-out end of the container for the rod that started everything.

Looking down at the cooling remains of the city, Danvers reconsidered the logic behind the Compound's placement. Maybe the Kamanti were trying to protect themselves from the humans, but the buildings were just far enough away to survive the kind of strike that destroyed Tuanach. The etchings on the cylinder dug into his palm as Danvers clutched it tight. He tried to crush it, remove all reminders of Last Light of Day and Brandiwicz's fate. But it was stronger than he thought. Looking down, Danvers realized perhaps he needed something to remind himself that he didn't have all of the answers. Finally, he turned his back on the sea of charred lava below; certain that even such a huge memorial to hubris would have very little effect on humanity in the long run.

BETWEEN SCYLLA AND CHARYBDIS

A tale of the 142ⁿᵈ Starborne

Patrick Thomas

AJOR HANS BENEDICT WATCHED THE ALIEN VESSEL APPROACH, FROM the point it first appeared as a dot in the distance, until it was finally close enough to block everything else from his sight.

It was time to get to work.

Waiting had been the easy part. The next step was tricky. The ship they dubbed *Magog* had ignored attempts to communicate as it headed directly for the human settlement on Kailash, but it had noticed small drones and reacted by dissolving them into their component atoms. Approaching it, even in something designed to look like space debris, didn't seem like a good idea. Which is why, as the best sapper in the 142ⁿᵈ Starborne, Benedict got the job. The fact that his superior officer General Daily believed it was a suicide mission didn't matter. Hans Benedict had never shirked his duty or disobeyed an order, not even when he fully expected to be vaporized into a cloud of atoms.

Behemoth's long-range sensors could not penetrate the hull, but had located what was assumed to be a clear viewport midway up the ship. Most Host warships limited viewports because of the risk of a hull breach, but they had several as a backup in case their sensors failed. For a ship the size of a large asteroid, it seemed odd to have only one, but Benedict was thankful for it. Otherwise, he wouldn't have a decent point of entry, assuming he lived long enough to make the attempt.

That single window was the target at which Benedict had launched his coffin, which is not as easy as it sounds. A coffin was basically just that—a sealed cylinder with windows, a minimal amount of air, and only an old-fashioned, hand-cranked radio for communications. No other technology to be picked up by the target's sensors and multiple liners to mask any life signs.

Not only did he have to figure his own trajectory, but that of the *Magog,* calculate where and when the two would meet and then wait. It was akin to shooting at a target that was out of range, then getting the bullet to stop and wait for the target to run into the bullet hours later. It was risky. One small miscalculation would insure that the gargantuan ship smashed him and his coffin to pieces, assuming he didn't get atomized first.

As soon as he was inside the range at which the earlier probes were disintegrated, he found himself gritting his teeth, waiting to be destroyed.

Benedict almost missed the target, but only almost. He had planned for his coffin to land in the middle of the lone window but he missed that mark. Half of his coffin was on the hull and the other half on the window. The coffin's hull had nodules that burst upon impact to release a thick paste that worked as a shock absorber and quickly hardened to adhere it to the alien ship.

It worked. Clad in a black spacesuit, Benedict emerged from the coffin and headed toward the window. He looked inside, wondering if all his planning would be ruined by someone inside looking out at the view. Fortunately, the room was empty. Quickly, he used a molecular cutter to carve a hole big enough for him to board the ship. Instead of glass or plastic, the window itself was made out of some sort of crystalline substance two feet thick. It was almost half an hour later when he pushed the cut section in and moved to the side as the chunk of window was shot outward by escaping gasses. Using specially designed boots and gloves, he managed to pull himself inside. Benedict quickly spun and placed a breach patch over his work. It wouldn't go unnoticed during a visual examination, but it did stop more of whatever passed for atmosphere in the ship from being lost to the vacuum.

After checking his patch work, Benedict crouched down and remained still as he assessed his surroundings. The atmosphere was remarkably similar to that of Earth, with lower nitrogen and higher oxygen and argon levels. Like Behemoth, the Magog had artificial gravity, although about ten percent higher that Earth normal.

Host ships had corridors and rooms built from pieces placed together in rectangular formations, but the alien ship, or at least the room he'd entered, seem to lack seams. The surface was covered with ridges and bumps similar to those formed by painted with a sponge.

Most importantly, Benedict saw no signs of life or any form of mechanical detection. He had hoped he wouldn't find any. Not just to make his job easier, but because of his orders. If the ship was abandoned, they would take it as salvage and learn as much as they could about its technology. However, if the ship was not running on automated sensors and had a crew, standard orders from the Sway government back on Earth were clear. Kill them all.

Two centuries may have passed since the Earth was last invaded, but those in power hadn't forgotten that the planet had only been saved by a fluke set of circumstances and the insight of one man, the same man who later would unite the planet under the Sway government. Their directive was clear. Any alien races or cultures encountered that appeared to have a higher technology level than the Sway must be destroyed in a show of force so as to discourage any thought of an attack on Earth or one of the colony worlds.

Benedict was a good soldier and would follow orders, then deal with the wounds to his conscience after.

His first guess that he was in an observation room seemed correct. There were lumps lining the floor, walls, and ceilings that might have been seats, as if whatever used them were not restricted to the floor. Maybe gravity for this room could be turned off.

Exiting the room was problematic. Examination of the room gave him the impression that it had been molded rather than assembled. There were no panels or tiles to open; no visible exit. Benedict continued to touch the wall and found a coin-sized area that could be pressed down. He heard a click and a circular opening appeared in the wall.

The corridor was cylindrical, with no flat surface to walk on. It took several steps for Benedict to adapt to walking on the curved surface. Like the observation room, the corridors had no noticeable seams. Scanners attached to his chest, back, and wrists took readings on everything, feeding the data to a contact in his left eye.

The *Magog* may have been resistant to *Behemoth's* external scanners, but now that he was inside he was able to detect several energy signatures, including one that was giving off enough juice to power a medium-sized city, but with no harmful radiation. If the Host could figure out how the ship was putting out that level of power, it might be a new energy source for all the colony worlds, making life for the settlers that much easier.

Through trial and error, Benedict started to recognize a slightly different impression for where the doors were. Each had a camouflaged disc that popped up when you pressed it. The switch had a hole in the center. Benedict needed to stick his finger in and turn counterclockwise as he pulled to have the doors open. The rest of the corridor doors were different than the first he encountered and were brilliant pieces of engineering. A circular portion of a wall opened as sections of the wall separated into individual rods that pointed from the outside toward an empty space in the center. The nearby parts of the doors wound around the rods not unlike an old-fashioned blind. They were not easy to walk through without being poked or jabbed, so Benedict got in the habit of holding onto two of the upper rods to lift himself up and swing himself through feet first.

Two hours later, as he approached the energy signal, he still had not come across any living beings or automations. The ship seemed in perfect working order, so it made no sense for its makers to have abandoned it.

When he turned the last open switch, a larger circular section of wall simply disappeared like at the observation room.

The second thing he noticed was the dead alien at his feet. The first was the individual tube-like chambers that stretched on for what looked like miles. Each had a view port made from the same crystalline structure as the hull window, allowing him to see inside.

Each tube contained the body of what he could only assume were members of the race that made the ship.

They were not humanoid.

Benedict's first impression was that the race that had built the *Magog* were storing some kind of seafood, at least judging by the appearance of the creatures, some sort of variation on the octopus or squid. Closer examination revealed significant differences. These creatures had ten tentacles, six serving as what he thought of as legs and four that might be considered arms. No fingers, no opposable digits, but what looked like an alternating mixture of suckers and single claws.

It was hard to tell for sure, but they looked like they had five of what passed for eyes spread over the front and sides of what was likely the head. He couldn't make out ears, nose, or a mouth for that matter. The creatures were long, wider at the bottom not unlike a bulbous umbrella.

For a civilization to make the effort to put this many of their people on a ship this advanced, there should have been some sort of internal defense or at least guards. Benedict kept waiting for an attack that never came.

As he continued his exploration of the bio-storage facility, he came across the likely reason for his lack of a reception. At least twenty of the creatures lay spread across the floor, dead, the purple flesh decaying off their bones. Although bones might not have been the right term. The skeletons looked thin and flexible, more like cartilage. Each alien corpse had holes cut clean through their bodies, but no incineration or energy burns. It was as if parts of their bodies had just ceased to be.

Still clad in his spacesuit, Benedict bent down to remove something from one of the dead creature's arm tentacles. It looked like a long, thick metal cylinder that had been sliced in half the long way. It had two bands that connected it to the tentacle and ended in a point. Each of the dead — Benedict decided to call them Magogians — wore two, each with slightly different markings and shades. They each gave off unfamiliar, yet distinct energy signatures.

Benedict's gut assumed they were weapons and he took several moments figuring out how they were triggered. The two holding rings that connected it to the tentacle had sensors. The Magogians must have been able to flex segments of their tentacles to press on both sensors at the same time. Benedict theorized that hitting them both at the same time would fire the weapon. It was dangerous and stupid to attempt, but he had to assume that whoever shot them was still alive and would come across him eventually. Without knowing their exact physiology, he could not be certain his sidearm would kill a Magogian, but these things likely could.

Holding the first weapon with the point out, the same way he found it on the tentacle, Benedict experimented. By hitting the closer sensor first, then the further one, it let out a glowing mist that seemed to ride on a beam of energy. He pointed it at one of the dead Magogians and pressed the sensors. The creature's flesh dissolved into a mist which then vanished, much like what had happened to the Host's probes. Extending the time between pressing the sensors built up a more powerful charge that made hunks of metal go away.

He picked up the second weapon. It was of a similar shape, but shorter and made of a darker metal. It had the same triggering sensors. He pointed it toward the floor and fired. A beam of energy shot out that melted the surface of the floor.

Benedict let out a short, surprised whistle. While the Host had energy weapons, they were mounted on ships because they hadn't been able to miniaturize them enough for a soldier to carry safely. The Magogians had obviously figured out how to make it work.

His contact lens screen flared to life and Benedict closed his left eye to see it better. There was a power surge not far from his location. He rushed to investigate, taking the energy weapons with him.

At the center of the surge, there was a living, moving Magogian standing in front of rows of glowing extrusions.

Benedict had his orders. He stepped out, planning to shoot the creature with the energy weapon, when the machine hummed and the glow suddenly expanded, enveloping both Benedict and the Magogian in a glittering nimbus.

The ship was gone. Benedict stood above a blue, living planet as the history of that world unfolded before him. He watched as the Magogians left their oceans, rose up and fell, built civilizations, created art, made love and war, and developed space travel. They went out to explore the universe, but did not colonize, choosing instead to learn. On one excursion, their ship discovered a dead world. Scientists gathered artifacts and brought them back to their world, which they referred to in their own language simply as Home, just as they referred to themselves as Us.

They set about trying to deduce what had destroyed the world they found. The idea of a planetary apocalypse disturbed them so much they set about building space arks, a way to make sure their race would survive even if Home did not.

It took years for them to complete the first ark and they had begun work on the second when tragedy struck. Their scholars had continued examining artifacts from the dead world and opened a book the scanners showed was bound with organic material, most likely some sort or dermis or skin.

The scholars tried to open their minds in hopes of deciphering what was written. One succeeded, then made the mistake of reading the text aloud.

Benedict watched in horror as the book opened a portal to a place of unspeakable darkness. Nightmares came through to destroy Home. The only good fortune was the completed ark lay on the far side of the world. Many Us—Benedict decided to change what he called them to Usian—panicked, but others came up with a plan. They could not stop the aliens, but they were able to slow their progress. Tens of millions, maybe more, brave Us did not hide or try to save themselves. Instead they fought against the nightmares destroying Home in an effort to hold back the dark invaders long enough for the ark to be filled with one million of their people and launched into space.

And through sheer determination, they succeeded. The ark now searched for a new home and its sensors had located a suitable world. The Us were essentially a compassionate people, so Benedict assumed they hadn't realized that Kailash was already inhabited by a human settlement or they would have kept looking. Explanations of the ship, its systems, the weapons, Usian biology, and even languages were downloaded into Benedict's mind.

He now knew how to maintain the status tubes, pilot the ship, and even some basic medical care for the Usians.

Then the images vanished and he was left feeling dizzy and for a moment like he had too few limbs.

The teachings he had absorbed had been comforting and made him forget for a moment where he was and what he was doing. The Usian who had triggered the knowledge device recovered faster and realized the human was behind him and lashed out with a rapid-fire blur of tentacles that stripped him of the energy weapon and knocked him, battered and bruised, to the floor.

The creature screamed at him with sounds that should have been incomprehensible to the human, but weren't.

"What be you and why you be here?" the creature demanded.

Benedict struggled with his vocal chords and tried to mimic the sounds needed to answer as he got to his feet and tried to back out of tentacle reach.

"Me Major Hans Benedict..." His name and rank was said in English as there was no equivalent and the Us had a different grammar structure. "...of the Host. Us ship is approaching We world. Please reverse course, leave system."

"World holds no true civilization."

"We have settlement."

"Barely any."

"One hundred thousand."

The creature trilled like a bird going through a food processor. It was a laugh.

"Over one million Us ride ark. Need ours greater than need yours."

Benedict knew the Us to be a determined people and the ark unable to achieve orbit again once it landed on a planet. The Usians would claim Kailash, likely the same spot the human settlement had, as it was the most hospitable to both races. Most Usians would offer to let the humans leave, but Benedict knew the human settlers would fight to the death before giving up the world they were making their own. Now that it was found that the ship was not abandoned, standing Sway government orders demanded that Benedict destroy the Usians and their ark.

For the first time in his career, Benedict hesitated. Having experienced what it was like to be one of the Us, even for a moment, left him loath to commit what amounted to genocide.

In desperation, Benedict tried logic. "Us hold lives blessed. Against slaughter."

The Usian laughed again. "Honor Protectors prattle same fools' speak. Want Us leave system to find another world to settle. Me old, fatigued from so many time wasted in search. World become ours. Me kill rest Protectors. Learner beam teach Me flying of ship. Land then awake rest Us. Will send to atoms others on world so Me finally rest."

"Lives be ended."

"Lives be restarted. Time for others to pass beyond, starting on you."

Responding to the death threat, Benedict pulled out his sidearm and fired at the Usain's center eye as he fled. He hit his fleshy target, barely slowing the mass of angry tentacles which sped after him, using the walls and ceilings instead of the floor.

The creature shot an energy beam and would have hit Benedict had he not zigged to the side, running full out toward the nearest status tubes. Once inside the large chamber, his tentacled attacker no longer had the high ground advantage, as the chamber was too enormous and the walls too far away from where Benedict ran. He fired at the Usian, wasting shots that did the tentapod little harm, until he ran out of ammunition.

The major scanned for weapons and found none. Instead he crouched to get his bearings behind a status pod, thinking himself safe, for the only way to shoot him now would be to take out another one of the Us.

An energy beam cut through the pod and its occupant, missing Benedict's head by inches.

The alien was beyond reason, willing to kill its own people to get at the sapper.

Running behind the chambers, Benedict headed back toward the nearest pile of bodies, energy beams destroying pods all around him.

He ran by an alien corpse, grabbing hold of the nearest weapon — one of the lighter, metal variety — and kept moving. The tentacle tore off so Benedict pulled it out of the rings and put his index fingers near the sensors and pressed the rear one. Aiming forward of where he estimated the last energy beam came from, he dove to the ground and hit the forward sensor, sending a dissolving beam of light and mist out.

Benedict kept moving. He assumed he hadn't hit his target or there would have been screaming.

Where the hell was that tentacled bastard?

He heard a clang and fired in that direction, realizing too late it was a ploy, the noise likely coming from something his opponent threw as a distraction.

Something grabbed his ankle, pulling him down and out from behind the pods. A second tentacle reached out and pulled something off the alien weapon in his hand. Benedict fired at point-blank range but nothing happened.

The Usian jiggled a metal piece from the hook on the end of his tentacle. "No power no work."

Another tentacle wrapped around Benedict's neck and lifted him off of the floor and into the air so his face and what passed for the alien's head lined up.

The alien laughed, then stopped as Benedict rammed the pointed end of the weapon through the fleshly area that would be a human's neck, but he now knew housed the alien's motor cortex. The medical training the beam had taught him included what areas were most important to stabilize in the event of injury. Coincidentally, those areas also made the best kill points. The alien murderer stiffened before sliding to the ground, its tentacle still wrapped around Benedict's throat.

Benedict pulled the limb off, gasping for air. "Still works pretty good I'd say."

He slid the combat knife off his belt and quickly stabbed several more vital areas to make sure the creature was truly dead.

He returned to his coffin to retrieve the explosives he had brought with him and spent the next ten hours placing them around the ship in what the learning beam had shown him were ship's most vital systems. Now having intimate knowledge of how their communications array worked, he could launch his coffin, radio for pick up, and detonate them remotely.

But these people were the last of their race. Slaughtering them while they slept in status was the act of a coward, not a soldier. And genocide was too horrible to contemplate. But if the Usians awoke and tried to take Kailash, even *Behemoth* couldn't stand against them for long.

There had to be another option. A way to get the Usians out of system and away from human settlements and have the general and the Host believe that the ship had been destroyed.

Benedict returned to the learning beam. Thanks to his prior exposure, he not only knew how to activate it, but how to have it teach him specific things. He needed to know about the status chambers and how the ship traveled between star systems.

A plan slowly came to him. He reprogrammed the ship, then evacuated via the coffin as the ship reversed course. It was quickly out of weapons range.

"Sapper One needs pickup," he said after cranking up the radio.

"Roger that, Sapper One. Harpy dropship is en route to your location."

A short while later Benedict was sitting in the dropship's cockpit with General Dailey on the view screen.

It was Major Hans Benedict's educated and personal judgment that General Dailey was a five-star idiot. Not that as a career man the major would ever repeat those thoughts aloud to anyone.

"Well, Major, what's the story? Is the ship salvage or a target?"

"Target, sir."

"Then why is it intact? And moving away from us?"

"I wanted a larger perimeter for safety."

"Why?"

As if in answer, there was an EMP burst, followed by the ship's disintegration weapons discharging a luminescent cloud instead of a beam.

A moment later the ship was gone.

Dailey's mouth fell open. "You reduced the entire ship to atoms? How?"

"It wasn't easy, turning the ship upon itself." Or at least giving the appearance of doing so. The electromagnetic pulse helped disguise the ship exiting the system. Benedict gambled that since the *Behemoth's* sensors didn't detect it until after it arrived in the system, the same would be true of *Magog's* exit. It was on its way to a system far down the Sway government list for colonization. There were currently three hundred worlds approved for consideration and fifty more that were suitable, but not ideal. He chose the best one off the second list that was on the outskirts of mapped space as it would not likely be colonized for at least a century, if at all.

The status chambers would open one hundred pods as they entered that system and those hundred Usians would be enough to prepare the rest of the ship for planet fall.

Benedict planned to file a report that he had information that this system was likely inhabited and have it delivered to the Host High Command after his death to prevent any surprises for future colonists. The Usians would be cannibalizing the *Magog* to rebuild themselves and would no longer be a space-faring threat and thus the standing order to destroy would not apply.

"You are confident that the *Magog* is no longer a threat to humanity?"

"I am, General." And he was. Major Hans Benedict was no one's fool. He was aware that something could happen and the ship might even return, but he had erased the *Magog's* sensor sweeps from the time period that he planted the bombs and all records of their time in the Indus system. Should the need arise, he could cripple or destroy the ship remotely.

He hoped it wouldn't, because his career would be over, but disobeying orders to save one million lives—the remains of an entire race and civilization—was the right thing to do. The honorable path to take.

"Meet me in command for a full debriefing as soon as you are back on *Behemoth*."

"Yes, sir."

As he disembarked the Harpy, he tripped and the pilot had to catch him.

"Careful, Major. Breaking in new feet?"

For a moment, Benedicts mind had been trying to walk with six tentacles instead of legs, causing him to trip.

"No, Captain. Breaking in the old ones."

THE STAR GAZERS

James Chambers

KHATE WINCED AT THE SIX-INCH, STEEL FRAGMENT PROTRUDING FROM HER thigh, and the blood welling onto her flight-suit. She should've grabbed the damn first aid kit when she wriggled free of the wrecked life boat. Retrieving it now meant crawling back over Jarn's corpse.

At least her mother's field pouch and its contents remained strapped to her waist thanks to her single-minded refusal to part with it. From the look of her wound, though, she needed the first aid kit more. The gash seemed deep enough for spray flesh but probably not life-threatening as long as she stanched the bleeding. The balance of her bruises, cuts, and burns hurt like hell but would heal well enough on their own. She wished Jarn had also come through the crash as safely and choked back a deep sob.

Electric humming alerted her to the return of the hover-assassins that had downed the boat.

Groaning, Khate lurched beneath an immobile fold of the nearby Star Gazer's robe and toppled into the enormous structure's shade. Salton metal in the Gazer would hide her from the HA's sensors. Jarn had sighted on the figure before the salvo that had blasted them from the sky, and the boat had come down only thirty meters away. She landed on her knees, skidding to cover. The shrapnel in her leg twisted, blasting agony through her adrenalin rush and tipping her into a gray fog. She lingered there, bleary and light-headed, until the squad of HAs, having detected no signs of life, departed.

Khate opened her eyes to empty sky.

Bracing herself on the warm base of the Star Gazer, she struggled upright.

Endless meadows of sere grass swayed around her in warm, half-hearted breezes. To the south awaited the planet's only city, Salton's Rig, her destination. To the east and west, lines of Star Gazers at thirty-seven kilometer intervals encircled Salton's equator. To the north, past the smoking wreck of the life boat, a sea of grass she knew gave way to desolate taiga near the pole, a haunted land filled with the ghosts of spent mines from her mother's first expeditions.

The decimated life boat slouched like an oryx chewed apart by jackals. Khate eased from the Gazer's shadow, watching, listening, but detecting no sign of the HAs. Every motion added fuel to the bonfires of pain burning in her body. The stink of machine blood and burned metal seared her nostrils. As she neared the boat, her body refused to take another step, overwhelmed by the fierce smell of her husband's charred flesh, by raw, sensory grief. She exhaled an apology to Jarn, her words warped into a keening dirge as they crossed her trembling lips. She had brought him here only to die as would countless others if she failed. She compartmentalized her despair the way her mother had taught her, the same way she had so many other losses on her path to this moment and saved it for mourning later — if later ever came.

Shutting her eyes, she crab-walked through the misshapen hatch. Radiant heat enveloped her. She covered her mouth and nose with one hand as the greasy, sour odor of Jarn's still-sizzling flesh flooded her nostrils. Touching him as little as possible she fished for the first aid kit, each second of groping the ruined console like a thousand days of torture, until her fingers found the hard plastic case and nudged it free. She pressed the kit to her chest and backed out, gagging, desperate for open air. Midway back to the shelter provided by the Gazer, she folded to her knees. Fresh agony flared in her thigh. She dry heaved and afterward collapsed and rolled onto her back, every limb buzzing with hurt.

High and far above, a nuclear blaze churned on Salton's mesospheric fringes, remnants of the transport ship that had brought her and Jarn here.

Its entire crew, all its passengers, except for her, sacrificed to bring her to Salton's Rig.

Hot tears spilled down her cheeks. Her mother's ways failed her, and she wept. Whether for Jarn, her pain, the dead and all those soon to die, or for all of it together, she couldn't say.

Beside her the 400-foot-high Star Gazer remained unmoved, poised eternally skyward. Its many eyes peered longingly at the heavens. One of its right limbs reached toward space, sleeve peeled back from a coiled appendage bristling with wiry tendrils. Motionless swaths draped from its knobby joints and slithery lashes, more like wings or fin membranes than robes, though that's what people called them, imparting a sort of reverence. Iridescence limned the enormous figure. Colors coruscated in its Salton skin. Waves cycled through the tall grass in rhythm to the shifting hues. So ripe with a sense of motion yet forever unchangeable, encapsulating the mystery of Salton metal. Power source. Weapon. Building material. Energy given form and substance. An enigma to which Khate possessed the answer no one wanted to believe. From here, the Gazer appeared to reach toward the burning scar of her dead transport, stretching to catch a dying ship that would never fall—or perhaps to deflect its unwanted intrusion.

Khate choked back a fresh wave of sobs, sat up, and snapped open the first aid kit.

Using the scissors, she snipped away part of her suit. The wound looked clean, but rich, dark-red blood still bubbled from it. She grabbed the spray flesh can in one hand, gripped the shrapnel with her other, and clenched her jaw. She eyed the strong analgesics in the kit but didn't dare ease her pain at the cost of dulling her reflexes. After a silent count to three, she yanked the sliver loose and released an anguished wail. She sealed the wound with spray flesh, antibiotic vapor cooling her skin then tickling as it dried and closed the gash.

She watched until the bleeding stopped and then crashed back on the grass.

Her pain dimmed to a constant, throbbing ache. She drew an energy bar from the kit and ate it, washing it down with a shot of electrolyte tea.

After a while, the sweat on her brow dried, and the persistent reek of death sickened her.

She unzipped her mother's pouch and confirmed it still contained the data chips of half a dozen Riggers who'd taken the flight to Endless. Each had come from a lost corpse drifting in its forsaken ship through one of the many debris clouds the war with the Infinite Empire had left scattered around the galaxy. Each held a razor's edge of truth, a testament to hubris. And each justified the lives she'd used, the fortune she'd exhausted to obtain them—but only if she could reach

Salton's Rig before morning and show them to her contact, whose people held enough power to act on their truth.

Jarn had intended to land them midway between Rig and the nearest Star Gazer, only twelve klicks away, but the hover-assassins drove them off course 100 kilometers out. Khate had no idea how far from the city they'd come down.

She zipped the pouch closed then rose and hobbled south, her gait steadying with every step. On the grasslands' western edge, twin suns hung low, emphasizing the urgency of her task. Night fell quickly on Salton. She walked until the stars emerged then used them to gauge her position. Rather than a dozen klicks to Rig, more than seventy lay ahead of her. On foot she could never reach the city in time. The realization gutted her.

To come so close only to fall so short.

Someone had betrayed her to Alann Thanh, and Thanh had responded as he'd sworn to if she ever returned. He hadn't yet killed her as promised, not directly, but if she couldn't make the city before dawn, she was as good as dead. She may as well retreat to the wrecked boat, lie down beside Jarn, and wait to die with everyone else.

Instead, she pressed southward, thinking of her mother a century ago.

Afloat in interstellar space, sustained only by basic life support, her ship's engines, comm systems, and weapons dead, Mina Salton had hurried through repairs, racing against starvation, dehydration, or asphyxiation that would almost certainly claim her before she completed them—when she drifted across the enigmatic empty ship made of Salton metal. The first discovered. She'd used it to get home then tracked down its abandoned origin world—the only known source of the metal—and reaped a fortune.

Hope never fails us, her mother used to say. *We fail hope when we release it before it's done with us.*

She died never knowing her discovery also handed humanity the keys to its extinction.

Night fell and the wind turned chilly. A fog of stars speckled the sky. Against the distant glow of Salton's Rig daubed onto clouds, ship lights danced.

Khate's leg throbbed. Her stomach grumbled.

The rhythm of grass and earth crunching underfoot mesmerized her.

When a cruiser buzzed out from the west, the proximity alarm in her bio-monitor warned her before she spied its approaching lights.

The tall grass offered only shadows for cover, so she flattened her body to the earth and hoped the cruiser pilot didn't see her. But the ship didn't fly over and vanish as she wished. It hovered for several seconds before the clank of landing skids deploying announced its descent less than fifty yards from her position.

Khate struggled to her feet and then ran, bolting south.

She ignored an amplified voice ordering her to stop. Grass and soil padded underfoot. Clicking, beeping, buzzing sounds followed her, until two hover-assassins floated in front of her face, their glaring lights outlining the guns aimed at her. The drones rattled off further demands for Khate to stop. She shrieked and swung the first aid kit, knocking one of the HAs to the ground with a crack and a shower of sparks.

"Hey! Watch it!" an amplified voice called. "You know how much it costs to repair those?"

Footsteps drum rolled after her. Khate spun to confront a figure whose face hid behind the lowered visor of a flight helmet. Beyond, the cruiser idled, its engines bright with Salton metal glow. The pockmarked hull indicated the flier belonged to a bounty hunter, scavenger, or another class of outcast, none of whom could mean Khate any good.

She snatched up the damaged hover-assassin and aimed its gun.

The figure skidded to a stop and raised its arms. "Whoa, whoa! Okay, okay, don't sweat the damage. I can probably fix it myself. Just point that another direction, will you?"

Khate ignored the request. "Helmet open, slowly."

The visor rose to reveal the soft face of a young man with delicate features, hair shaved to the scalp, pilot's anti-glare smudge rimming his gently slanted eyes. Khate detected an odd mix of fear and hope in his expression.

"I'm Slinnmath Raychan. You can call me Slinn," he said. Un-amplified by his helmet, his voice sounded warm and young. "Are you Khate Salton?"

"Don't worry about who I am. How old are you?" Khate said.

"What? What the hell does that matter?"

"You don't look old enough to fly the Gazer trail, let alone own a cruiser. Who's in your flier waiting to jump me?"

"Oh, I get it. No one." Slinn shrugged. "I may be young, but I fly better than most people twice my age. So why not fly the Gazers? I inherited the cruiser."

"Is that so? I'm going to have to take it from you," Khate said. "I need to be in Salton's Rig tonight."

"Yes, I know. That's why I came for you. I'll take you to Rig."

Khate pulled back. "You came looking for me?"

"The Gazers told me you'd be here. They said Thanh would try to kill you and fail, and I should look for you in the grasslands tonight."

"What do you mean the Gazers told you? No, forget it." Khate menaced Slinn with the damaged drone. "You're lying. Key card, now. I'll fly myself."

The *click-hum* of a weapon to her left gave her a chill and she froze.

"Shoot me, my other HA shoots you." Slinn nodded to the second drone which floated above Khate's shoulder, its gun-barrel eye focused on her head. "You realize I could've killed you without even landing if that's what I wanted, right?"

Khate hated to trust any stranger on Salton, but if he would bring her to Rig then maybe this was her reward for keeping hope. She lowered the damaged HA. The other ramped down its weapon and backed off.

"Fine, then, you drive," she said.

She tossed the broken drone at Slinn's feet and stalked toward the cruiser. Slinn retrieved his property then caught up and ushered Khate onboard. They soon lifted off to an altitude which offered a clear view of the lights at Salton's Rig and the eternal glow of the Star Gazers east and west of them. Slinn piloted with skill equal to his claim.

Khate studied his sincere eyes intent on flying, his narrow lips and soft cheeks, the face of a painter, poet, or musician but not a pilot flying the Gazers, fighting other scavengers for the meager bounty of erosion-shed Salton metal scales.

"How'd you inherit this ship?" she asked.

"My uncle left it to me. I dropped out of university and came here to accept it. He's the one who taught me to fly. I've been flying the Gazers almost a year. The dreams started right away."

"What dreams?"

"It's how the Gazers talk to me. Well, not *talk* exactly. They send me impressions or put me into other, ah, consciousnesses to experience. It's hard to explain. I kind of assumed you had the dreams too. I mean, you know more about the Gazers than anyone else. They're not what we think, are they?"

"No," said Khate.

A satisfied grin brightened Slinn's face. "I knew it!"

"What do you think you know?"

"They're alive, right? Salton metal, this whole planet is sentient."

Khate sighed. "You don't even know what you don't know."

"Yeah, well, I know how to fly, and I know to thank someone who picks my ass up from the grasslands and gives me a ride."

Khate rested her head on the seat back. "Thank you for the ride, know-nothing Slinn."

Engine thrum filled the silence between them.

They passed the next Gazer en route to Rig. Its monstrous face and myriad eyes regarded them with unblinking indifference reflecting multiples of distant flickering fire. Khate glanced upward to the wreck of her transport, an extra star in the night burning hotter and brighter than Salton's rising moon.

"How do you know your dreams come from the Gazers?" Khate asked. "Couldn't they be from your subconscious?"

"Collective subconscious, maybe. I'm not the only one who dreams them. A dozen of us dream pieces of the same dreams then decode them collectively, piece together all the separated things. We dream fragments of cities with towers and great halls that defy geometry. Streets that entwine infinitely on themselves. We visit sunken places where light doesn't exist, yet somehow we can still see. I was in art school when my uncle died so I draw. Others write, make music, or sculpt. The planet wants us to understand it."

"The Gazers tell you that?"

"Why else would they communicate? They need us to explain them to others."

"Assuming I even buy that, how do you know you can trust the dreams?"

"They brought me to you, didn't they?"

"There are other ways you could've known to look for me," Khate said. "People in Rig know I'm coming. I've already been betrayed once on this journey."

Slinn shrugged. "I guess."

Rig drew closer, brighter, an unchecked tumor of metal, glass, plastic, and commerce. It remained so much smaller in Khate's memory, no more than a cluster of temporary shelters, and steel building skeletons, and roads that existed only on maps. She knew it best that way, at its beginnings, her childhood home where her mother led the Salton mining efforts, and ships of all kinds brought workers and equipment and took away tons of Salton metal bound for shipyards orbiting Cluster, Nyad, Galapagos, and other worlds. All for the war effort. Every ounce of cargo still increased her family's fortune. Khate had spent her share as fast she accrued it until she'd stooped to borrowing from Jarn to make the last leg of her journey back here.

"You can't dock at the port. I'll be found," she said.

"The Gazers showed me it'll be fine. Thanh thinks you're dead."

"I don't care what you dreamt. Set down by the eastern market near the med plaza. It'll be desolate this time of night."

Glittering lights and shifting shadows expanded to fill the view screen. Constant motion. Boundless energy. Ships rising and falling by the immense spaceport she had never seen before. So much had migrated to the realm of pure memory. Khate wrung her scarred hands.

The cruiser slowed for approach.

She squeezed Slinn's arm. "Didn't you hear me? Approach from the east."

"Relax. This is the best way."

"No, turn this thing around now!"

Slinn shook his head. "My cruiser, my choice. Salton wants it this way."

Khate grabbed Slinn's wrist and yanked, trying to pull it from the control board and force a course change, but he proved stronger than she. Status lights flashed when Rig's flight control system locked onto the cruiser, and the small ship's flight computer defaulted to auto-pilot. Any change now would draw immediate pursuit from manned security patrollers. Khate weighed her options. Fight Slinn, seize the cruiser, and run. Hide on board and try to slip into Rig unseen. Or place her trust in Slinn and his dreams and hope for the best.

The cruiser entered the landing zone, drifting to a docking platform quicker than she'd expected. She decided on hope. It had brought her this far.

Outside, a standard flight crew converged on the craft.

No sign of HAs, city police, or of Thanh's Special Mining Guard.

"See?" Slinn said. "We can walk right in."

Khate waited a little longer. Nothing out of the ordinary appeared on the dock.

She and Slinn barely merited notice from the bustling crew when they debarked to the flight way and entered the space port.

"I have to go to the Okama Building in the med plaza," said Khate.

"We can get rail transport down here." Slinn directed Khate to a fork in the corridor but then hung back as she rounded the first curve. "The thing is, Ms. Salton, the Gazers have given us so much we have to trust them now and do what they want, and they don't want you to go to the Okama Building."

"What?" Khate heeled around. "What do you mean?"

Ahead a scuffle of feet pattered. Men in Mining Guard uniforms rushed at them. Khate swore at Slinn then shoved past him, heading back toward the dock, but guards came from that direction too and blocked her way.

She punched Slinn in the chest, knocking him against the wall. "Idiot! Liar!"

"Trust the Gazers," he said. "Everything will be fine. Better than fine. Wonderful!"

The guards encircled them. Slinn joined two officers who pressed through the ranks.

A familiar and unwelcome voice boomed down the flight way. "I swore to kill you if you came back here. You've been gone so long, I never expected I'd have to make good. Why'd you do it, Khate? Why return?"

The guards parted for Alann Thanh.

The gray-haired man stood nearly a head taller than the others, his face textured by years of worry and sunlight. He had lost nothing of his strength or posture. The sight of him unwound Khate to her ten-year-old self. Playing with dolls in the grass. Lifting her head to watch him walk in from the mines with the setting suns at his back after a day running the northern rigs. Mother calling from inside their housing module, hushing her away until he shucked his mine suit and washed up. An ocean of time between them that seemed to have passed in a sudden torrent. Only his hair's deep gray streaks and the faint droop at his left eye's corner broke the spell.

"I came to stop you killing every human in the known universe, Father," Khate said.

Her stature grew as she spoke, strengthened by her words. Rifles wavered in the hands of a few guards. Her father frowned.

"You've been crowing disaster since before I exiled you, yet we continue mining, living, thriving, despite all your Cassandra's tears. Your mother would—"

"*She* would be proud of me. Would've looked at the evidence and decided on the facts. She never would've shunned me for asking questions and pursuing the answers, no matter how much she didn't like them or how improbable she judged them."

Thanh sighed. His gaze moving over Khate, lingering at the pouch strapped to her waist.

"That belt belonged to her," he said.

"One of the few things of hers you let me keep."

"I've missed you all these years, Khate. Not a day passes I don't think of you and wish things were different. It's good to see you. I doubt you'll believe me, but it troubles me deeply how worn and aged you look. Whatever keeps us apart, I'm still your father. I sent you away to avoid hurting you or anyone else for that matter."

"Tell that the people on the transport you destroyed. Tell it to my… my husband's burnt corpse lying in wreckage on the grasslands."

Thanh shut his eyes and exhaled deeply. "I'm sorry, Khate. So very sorry. Their blood is on your hands, though. Along with those of the men and women you were to meet tonight at the Okama building. You knew the cost of returning to Salton, yet you chose to rope these people into your delusions. I must protect the trade. I must supply the war effort. Far more lives than theirs are at stake."

"They were already as good as dead." Khate fought hot tears and tried to believe her own words. "All of us are if you don't listen to me."

"Then speak now. I'm listening."

"You're opening six new mines. Don't! Keep them offline. You don't know what you're really digging into. I promise you that. You *don't* know. But I can show you."

"I knew you returned because of the mines." Thanh rubbed his forehead. He glanced at the guards, all hanging fire with expressions of nervous fascination. "If I keep them offline what of the fortune our mines provide which funded your years running from star to star? What of our struggle against the Infinite Empire if the Salton metal supply ends? How many will die if our defenses are weakened? Millions? Billions?"

"It'll be far fewer than if you bring those mines online."

"An outrageous claim! Where is your evidence of such a calamity, Khate? Where are the answers you've spent your life seeking?"

Khate unzipped her mother's pouch, scooped out the data chips, and showed them to her father. "Here. From half a dozen veteran pilots who flew a mission to Endless."

A quiet, collective inhalation passed through the guards, the officers, even Slinn. Thanh studied his daughter's face. Khate saw a crack in his façade, a glimmer of curiosity she had not seen there since childhood. She clutched tighter to hope that no longer seemed futile.

"Pilots who fly to Endless never return," Thanh said.

"I went searching for them."

"They never return *for a reason*, Khate. Prolonged exposure to Salton energy in a flight configuration affects one's mind. The mission to Endless is the last act of heroes before they turn dangerous to those they're sworn to protect. Whatever is recorded on those chips you ripped out of their brains isn't likely to even make sense."

"They're heroes, true. They protected us. Not from what they'd become but from what they feared they would set free."

"Stop being obtuse, Khate. Make your point."

"Look at them. Decide for yourself. That's all I ask."

"If I do and disagree, I'll have to keep the promise I made. It's my duty to protect the mines. If you don't convince me, you'll…well, I'll bury you beside your mother."

"Do you promise to act as decisively if you do agree?"

Thanh nodded. "You have my word."

Khate spilled the data chips into his open hand. He signaled for the guards to stand down then offered Khate his arm. She took it reluctantly and walked beside him to a waiting car with Slinn and four guards. A childish urge to hold his hand summoned dusty memories of walking with him to scout new mines and camps on the grasslands, and her nostrils filled with the stored scent of drying sweat and grass pollen. Her mother's laughter echoed faintly in her memory, and her father's young smile flashed across her thoughts. She unhooked her arm and slid into the car.

After a short trip, Thanh ushered Khate into a gallery at the Mining Commission. The guards waited outside. A replica Star Gazer dominated the gallery. A dozen men and women sat on loungers and chairs in its shadow. All eyes turned toward Khate and her father. When Slinn took his place among them, Khate guessed they were his fellow dreamers.

The gallery included an entire wall dedicated to Khate's mother's artwork. The sight of it nearly stole her breath. It seemed her father had gathered almost every piece her mother created, even some Khate had last seen in museums on Earth, or Mars, or Navroxen. Scintillating colors glittered from neo-organic canvasses and nanometer-thin sheaves of copper and platinum, the first Salton metal art ever created. Khate had never seen so many of her mother's works in one place. They bored a small, cold hollow in her, not only for the sense of loss they amplified but for their collective echo of all she had seen on the salvaged data chips. It occurred to Khate her mother had known—or at least intuited—much more than either understood.

The other walls showcased newer, less beautiful art. Relief sculptures. Cultured biofilms. Stardust collages. Dendral wood mosaics. Even handwritten pages of poetry and prose. The work of Slinn's dreamers Khate guessed, puzzle pieces created from fragmented dreams, glimpses of awareness too large for any single person to decipher.

"Slinn told you about the dreamers," Thanh said.

Walking the gallery wall, Khate nodded. "He didn't tell me they're working with you."

"The planet communicates through them. It communicated with your mother. She didn't understand it, but you can see it manifested in her art. No one knew it back then, but now people have lived here long enough to make sense of what they experience. We're learning the planet's language. It guides us, Khate, through the dreamers. The new mines are right where it asked us to build them. They're not going to harm Salton. All will be in a new type of harmony. We're partners now, humans and planet working together."

Slinn pointed to a triptych of paintings on ferrous glass. "These are my contribution."

"This planet is not alive," Khate said. "It's not even a goddamn planet."

Shocked silence blanketed them. All the dreamers stared at Khate with the lacerating pity reserved for those who have lost their senses.

"Khate, be reasonable," said Thanh.

"View the data. Look at the proof. I still have friends in the Mining

Commission. I know the mines come online at dawn so there's time left to make the right choice."

"All right," Thanh said. "Let's get this over with."

Thanh and Khate moved to a room off the gallery. Thanh thumbed the chips into a tray where they glowed when connected to the system. He keyed in several codes. Darkness spilled around them transforming the room into empty space, twinkling stars everywhere.

"Khate, as long as we haven't looked at these, I can spare your life. We can send you to a psych facility, restore your senses. No one will begrudge me a bit of mercy for my daughter, not while I control the Salton metal trade. Reneging on a vow will make me look weak for a while, but my reputation will recover. If we look at your data and it changes nothing, though, you'll have tied my hands. It will have been a tacit attempt to interfere with the war effort under false pretenses. I'll have to...You'll be executed as a traitor. Khate, I don't want—."

Khate laughed.

"The universe doesn't care what you want," she said.

"All right then. Show me."

Khate punched a final command into the viewer. The room melted. The walls dripped and folded around them and gave way to the vastness of space. A montage of flashing stars and far-off, pastel planets plunged them into a kaleidoscope. The walls and ceiling resolved into six discreet feeds unraveling the lives of six fighter pilots, all accelerated to the point of subliminal impression. The projectors scanned Khate's and Thanh's eyes and brains. Algorithms optimized the display for maximum comprehension in the shortest length of time. Years of experience danced across the screens, a mash-up of spaceflights, military bases, and combat missions. Short-lived explosions of enemy and friendly ships alike blotted out the stars. The perceptions of six men and women committed to duty, their mission hardly ever broken by distraction, punctuated only by infrequent revelry in officers' bars and furtive couplings between sorties; their lives like flares burning hot, bright, and fast; their minds loaded with stubborn rage for the enemy, the Infinite Empire, the endless adversary—and then space around them changed.

Thanh recoiled to the center of the room. One after another each display embarked on the flight to Endless. Pitch black space gradated to an oily, colorful sheen swirling in vortexes. Holes formed and widened, pressed stars aside, and devoured planes of empty void with the creeping vibrancy of Salton metal. Reality fragmented into geometric absurdities. Planets swelled, burst, and then contracted. Stars exploded and their pieces floated in fractal clouds of kinetic potential. Six times over, the universe tore itself down, reordered itself, and created something new.

Khate had seen this all before and couldn't bear to see it again. She focused on Thanh.

Thanh's mouth hung open, and tears poured from his eyes. The colors painted prismatic snakeskins on his face.

Convergence arrived. The moment when each pilot—altered by Salton metal—truly saw the universe, glimpsed the metal's purpose, and sensed the malevolent presence it held in check. A sub-audible cacophony invaded the room, a rabble of chaos unheard but felt in Khate's bones, accompanied by deathful whistling. The things the pilots saw reached into their minds softened by exposure to Salton metal to sway them to help it, to free it, to open its way into to a universe it intended to devour—and they fled to Endless to resist.

Blood thundered in Khate's head. Her heart lost its rhythm.

Thanh stumbled. Gasping, Khate touched his arm. He shrieked and threw himself against the control station, killing the display.

The room returned to normal.

Unable to look his daughter in the eye, Thanh asked, "What... what is it?"

"It's what's inside Salton. This planet isn't alive, not even a real planet. It's a prison built to contain them. All these years, we've been chipping away at it. It's not the planet sending dreams but its prisoners. The more we dig, the easier it is for them to reach us. Like the pilots who flew the Endless. The Salton metal softened their minds so these things could reach in and manipulate them. But they resisted, thinking they'd cracked up from trauma. And if the dreams showed you where to place the new mines then that's where they want them so they can break loose."

Thanh knelt before Khate and grasped her hands. He tried to speak, but his lips only trembled for several seconds before he found his voice. "I'm so sorry for not listening. For not trusting you. For making things worse."

Khate helped her father to his feet, his body shuddering beneath her hands.

"There's time to fix that now," she said.

A scream came from the gallery, followed by a thunderous crash. Khate and her father shared a questioning glance and then Khate opened the door onto a dozen dreamers gone berserk. Several tore down the artworks they had created from the walls, while others fought and choked each other. One lay dead on the floor, her head a puddle of blood and bone and muscle debris as if her skull had exploded from within. Slinn clambered over the replica Star Gazer, hammering its eyes with a length of steel scrap.

"What did you do?" Khate asked her father.

He grabbed her hand and rushed her from the gallery to an adjoining room with a view of Rig and the nearest Star Gazer to the east.

"My spies tracked you all the years you were gone, Khate," Thanh said. "They told me everything you did and hoped to accomplish. I couldn't risk you making trouble here. I couldn't endanger the war effort or risk the new mines."

The building rumbled and shook.

"I knew you'd try to stop us," said Thanh.

Outside, the nearest Star Gazer shifted. Its enormous bulk rose, split apart then shed itself in glowing chunks that rained down on the grasslands. Its many eyes and limbs, and the folds of its membranous robes disintegrated, spewing a cloud of color toward the night, gathering with polychromatic bursts from other Gazers. The aurora made it seem every Gazer had cracked and now divulged its toxic colors upward, obliterating the starlight and the burning stain of Khate's lost transport. The kaleidoscope sky swirled and bubbled then lacerated the night blackness.

A gargantuan, inhuman eye peered through. The gash widened. A second eye joined it, then others. Khate felt child-like, lost, and adrift. His eyes stark with fear, her father looked like no one she knew.

"Tell me what you did," Khate said.

Thanh held her by the shoulders as the world quaked. She focused on memories of her mother's voice, whispers from better days, on boxing away her terror, and not releasing hope.

"I brought the new mines online three days ago."

As gravity broke and maddening colors swarmed her, Khate clung to her father and refused to fail.

GIRAFFE CHILDREN

Robert E Waters

Standard Star Year 2434, *Geneva* Colony

He was Gomai. No, he was human. It was hard to know what he was, though his mother told him time and again, "You are human." It was one of his earliest memories. "And your name is Michael Jace Dickson, after your great-grandfather."

There was never any doubt.

Michael climbed from bed, a small, narrow cot that he had gotten used to in his seven years with Mother. She was an important lady in *Geneva* colony, so he had a cot and a comfortable room. Many others did not, and that didn't seem fair to Michael, though he didn't know how to complain about it. Other boys and girls like Michael didn't complain either. They were all treated differently than other human children. Special. Unique.

No, I'm human! It was hard to remember. He didn't *feel* human.

The dome was dark. He had a seahorse night light that let him see his way through the room. He tested the airlock. Closed, but not locked. What did Mother have to worry about? Her little man was human after all. He turned the lock and opened it, letting the pressure settle like he had done a thousand times. The circular door opened outward with a hiss. Michael let it slide out of the way and then stepped through the opening, onto a tiny walkway which led to their kitchen.

Humans could not smell *Geneva* grass, but Michael could. Right through the hab's protective dome. It was faint, but he could smell it. It called to him, that rich, flavorful smell that he had enjoyed on his free time outside. Humans couldn't go outside without layers upon layers of protective wear.

The other airlock opened just as easily, and Michael slipped through into the dark kitchen. It was a small space, the smallest in the hab besides the place where he expelled his waste. Mother was sleeping in her room just beyond the kitchen. She needed her rest; it had been another long day for her and the committee. Supplies were running low, and gathering edible grass in the fields of *Geneva* was proving to be harder and more costly than first expected. Only children like him could cultivate grass without danger of death, but like children, they preferred to play than to work. Those colonists who insisted that these special human children be put to labor instead of play were met with resistance and ridicule. Tensions in the colony were high.

Michael was tall for his age, and despite being told that he was a normal human, he had a longer neck than other human children. Those like him also had a longer neck, and some of them had elaborate patterns of patchy, polka-dot fur running down their backs. Michael did not, and he was glad of that, though jealous too. The patches gave those kids a status among the special children and a better understanding of who they were. But it wasn't supposed to be that way. Though the human adults never spoke about it around their special children, Michael sensed that something was wrong. Something had gone wrong with them, but he couldn't understand what it was. Michael longed for that understanding. "You were the first," Mother had told him. "The first what?" he had asked, but she had never explained.

He found the knife where Mother left it, in the sink, unclean. They had had potatoes and carrots for dinner from the small insulated garden that Mother had attached to the side of the hab. Nothing more than tough roots, really, for human produce did not grow well even in treated *Geneva* soil, but Michael tried never to complain. The knife felt big and awkward in his hand. He looked at his hand; he could see better in the darkness than Mother, and somehow that was okay. He had a human's hand. It just didn't feel like one inside.

He gripped the knife and went to Mother's room.

She never locked her door. She was a kind, trusting human. She had always treated Michael fairly. "You are my son, and I love you." He understood what love meant; at least he thought he did. He loved playing with the other children like himself. He liked being outside, breathing *Geneva* air, running through the grass, seeing groups of Gomai in the distance. They never seemed to want to get too close to the hab, nor have their children play with him and the others. He was sad about that, but he would take care of that later.

Michael opened Mother's door. She was nothing but a still lump beneath her sheets. She was facing the wall away from him, snoring. Michael smiled. He liked it when Mother snored. It was such a funny sound, and one that he couldn't make, try as he might. Apparently, his throat was not suited for such sounds; his longer neck made his snoring more of a high-pitched whistle. And he preferred that high-pitched whistle than speaking; it was easier to talk to the other children through those whistles than using human speech.

You are human, Michael. Everyone tells you that.

Not for long.

He crept across Mother's room, the knife in his hand, the blade pointed forward. Mother's snoring grew louder, more defined. She was dreaming deeply, he figured, and Michael wished he could see her dreams. He could see the dreams of the other children like himself, and they had decided that tonight was the night. It was time, and as much as Michael didn't want to do it, it was necessary.

He stood over his Mother's sleeping form. He let a tear drop from his left eye. A very human thing to do.

He lifted the blade. He gripped it harder than anything he had ever gripped in his life. He heard the voices of the other children in his mind, and he agreed. It was time.

Michael drove his knife into Mother's stomach, again and again, and whispering the words he had always wanted her to hear, to understand.

"I am not human. I am Giraffa."

Seven Years Earlier...

Colony Geneticist Milton Long could see the growing impatience in Mayor Marie Dickson's eyes. He ignored it and tried focusing on the images of tiny clusters of genes, sitting side by side, magnified a thousand times on the overhead display. One cluster human and the other Giraffa. The display was for the mayor's benefit, though Long figured that Dickson couldn't understand any of it.

"What am I looking at here, Milt?"

Long smiled. "Complex clusters of chromosomes, Marie. Chromosome 6, in fact, which houses the HLA genes...the human leukocyte antigens." He pointed to the clusters on the left. "These are human—" he pointed to the right, "—and these are Giraffa."

"Gomai, Milt," Dickson said, her eyebrows raised. "They are called Gomai."

The colonists had started calling them Giraffa because they had elongated necks and a pattern of neatly defined furry spots running the length of their spines, just like a giraffe. Long had gotten used to calling them that too, but Mayor Dickson didn't like the nickname, and made sure everyone knew it. He nodded in acknowledgement of his error. "Sorry. Gomai. HLA genes help to differentiate a body's own proteins from those created by bacteria or viruses. In short, they help to define and fortify a human's immune system. The Gomai have a similar cluster of genes, which I am calling Chromosome g6, for lack of a better term."

He waited to see if Mayor Dickson would comment. She didn't.

"Now," he continued, "between humans, these gene clusters can be quite different. That's why you have people with better immune systems than others, and why some have autoimmune diseases and others don't. It's just the way that we have evolved. The Gomai, as you might expect, are different." He shuffled through papers on his desk and pulled out a plain white sheet with columns and rows of numbers and double-helical patterns. Notes had been scribbled in the margins. "We have taken samples of dozens of Gomai, and although there are small differences between the core protein strands from one to another, they all possess this DNA strand here that serves as a blocker to any and all invasive proteins. Simply put: the Gomai immune system has evolved to continually adapt to its environment's changing volatility. It's an iron barrier. It's a better, more refined immunity than our own. In time, our immune systems could possibly adapt. But we don't have that kind of time, do we, Mayor Dickson?"

He knew the answer to that question. He was being smug and disrespectful for bringing up what they had discussed many times before. But he didn't care. Now he had the science to back up his argument.

Marie's expression turned pale. She breathed deeply, shook her head, and sat down. She rubbed her face, seemed deep in contemplation. "Is there no hope that we can adapt to this environment?"

Long shook his head. "Not without longer exposure. But as you have witnessed, any exposure at all has been deadly. We've lost 35 colonists, Marie, and some of them with environmental gear on. In order to adapt to any ecosystem, at least one person must survive contact for her immune system to adapt. Then another, and another, and on and on and on. That has not happened yet, and how many more can be sacrificed to see how long it will take? We're running out of options…and bodies."

To even acquire the DNA samples from the Gomai, they had to be captured in cages like animals, then dragged into one of the habitat's airtight holding bays where the sample could be taken. Even that extremely cautious procedure had killed two on Long's staff. All the Gomai used for the samples had died, despite Long's pain-staking efforts to keep them alive.

"What are the options?"

Long shrugged. "From my perspective, we have three. We keep living as we are, in these hab domes, and hope that our supplies and equipment hold out long enough for our immune systems to evolve naturally. Or, pack up the ship and find a more hospitable planet. Or, we gene splice portions of their g6 Chromosome into human embryos and see what happens."

Mayor Dickson spit. "Gha! Our supplies won't last another ten years, and I'll be damned if I ask these people to get back on that ship. They've sacrificed enough on that score. *Geneva* is perfect. The right climate. The right oxygen levels. The right gravity. The soil can be cultivated, and the flora is edible if treated properly. It's perfect, if only we didn't have to breathe its infectious air, filled with all those bacterial contagions that our immune system cannot handle. No, we can't leave. We've wandered space long enough. We must stay and make it work."

Long wanted to speak, but thought better of it. No sense pushing the matter any further. He had said his piece. Now it was Marie's decision…and the committee's.

She took a while to say anything. Long could see the agony of the decision on the mayor's taut face. She was a young woman, but the burdens of authority had begun to grey her hair. He could not remember the last time she laughed.

"Okay," Mayor Dickson said finally. "I'll discuss it with the committee. What are the risks?"

Long shrugged. "There are always risks when taking on the role of God, Marie, if you'll allow me a religious reference. But the basic structure of our chromosome and theirs is relatively compatible, from what I can see. At the worst, the human host will simply reject the splice. I foresee no long-term trauma."

Mayor Dickson raised an eyebrow. "You don't seem very confident, Milt."

Long shook his head. "Oh no, I'm confident that splicing can be done, and successfully. There are just a few strands of noncoding DNA within the Gomai sequence that I have to keep an eye on."

"Noncoding?"

"Junk DNA, in layman's terms. It doesn't encode protein sequences, so it's useless. Old genetic material that was once useful perhaps, but is now just taking up space. Humans have it as well. Harmless, but it'll be necessary to monitor it for due diligence."

"Okay, then who will be your first victim?" Mayor Dickson asked, apparently trying to lighten the mood.

Long shook his head. "We have to think long-term here. We can't splice an adult with an adult. By the time a Gomai becomes an adult, their immune system is baked. It becomes too strong by then, and it will kill the human host. It'll be like an auto-immune disease on steroids. Think Guillain-Barré syndrome, only ten times worse. But, like human babies, their juvenile immune systems are still developing. That's where we do the splicing. We splice human embryos with Gomai embryos."

Mayor Dickson sighed. "I was just telling you that our supplies will not last ten years. We need an immediate solution, Milt."

"We don't have one. We're going to have to hold out long enough for newborns with an improved immune system to become the basis by which we survive on *Geneva*. They can then live and thrive in the environment, and while we still live, they can scavenge for us, take care of us, until we pass on."

"So, what you are saying is that this habitat that we've constructed will serve, in the end, as our nursing home. Our grave."

Long shrugged. "Is it any different than anywhere else humans have lived? We're born. We grow up. We breed. We live. We die. This is just a different context than we are used to."

"I can't ask our families to give their babies over to this."

"Then, pack your bags, crank the engines, and let's hit the star road again."

The silence was cutting. Long could see the anguish in Mayor Dickson's eyes. The mayor paced, folded her arms, and looked through the broad window toward *Geneva's* golden-red veldt that rolled into the distance for miles. Long had to admit, it was a beautiful planet. It would be a shame to leave.

Finally, Mayor Dickson nodded. "Okay. If you are sure there will be no long-term risk."

"We're pretty good at genetic engineering these days, Marie. I think it'll work. It'll take time. But in the end, we'll be able to stay here, and end our roaming for good."

The mayor stared out the window once more. Long joined her and together, they watched a group of Gomai on the perimeter of the hab pause to feed on the long rubbery shoots of the indigenous grass. They were cultivating it for later as well, stuffing pawfuls into satchels hanging from their round shoulders. Long smiled. A nice, docile race. A kind of proto-Neanderthal, rising in capabilities, but still very limited. A perfect candidate for splicing. *The best chance we have*, Long thought. *The only chance.*

"Very well," Mayor Dickson said, turning to him and offering her hand in agreement. "We'll give this a try. But I won't ask families to volunteer. I will do this. I will donate my own eggs, and then if it succeeds, perhaps others can participate. But if not, no one else will have to suffer but me."

Standard Star Year 2434, Geneva Colony

Milton Long counted the bodies again, all laid out and ready for processing by the colony's lone crime-scene investigator.

"Seven total," Officer Williams said, as if he could read Long's thoughts. "All twelve children escaped, however. Some of them attempted to murder their mothers, but failed. Some chose not to do it at all and just fled. But they are all gone. Murderers and accessories to murder, all out there somewhere, in the wide *Geneva* savannah."

Long was only half-listening to the officer, as his eyes were fixed upon Mayor Dickson's pallid, yet serene, face. Her death hurt the most.

"Are there any clues as to where they might have gone?" Long asked.

Williams shook his head. "Not at this time, but judging from the lines of trampled grass from each hab that lead to one point, I'd say they all met after the fact, and then fled together."

Assistants to Officer Williams covered Mayor Dickson's body with a sheet and readied her for autopsy.

"What's the purpose of autopsies?" Long asked. "We know the cause of death."

"We're not looking for cause of death," Williams said. "We're looking for pathogens, which you should fully understand. If the children infected them in some way, the bodies will have to be burned."

All my fault... All of this was Long's fault. He'd been the one to recommend the gene-splicing to Mayor Dickson, and she had (grudgingly, perhaps) volunteered to be the first. He remembered her words: *no one else will have to suffer but me.*

That wasn't true by a long shot. But why? Why had they done it? And who was leading them?

That last question was obvious.

"Will you be going after them?"

Williams nodded. "Once I get enough volunteers."

"It's risky, and you know it."

"I know, but they murdered seven of our citizens, Long, including the mayor. We have to try to rein them in."

"I have to go with you," Long said, rising from a crouch. "We have to at least find Michael Jace."

Williams seemed confused. "Why?"

Long swallowed, took a deep breath, then said, "Because he is my son."

DATE: 2428

LOCATION: HUMAN COLONY 01

PLANET: GENEVA

FROM: PERSONAL LOG OF MILTON SANFORD LONG (`Classified, ALPHA-BRAVO 324)

MICHAEL JACE DICKSON WAS BORN TODAY, AT 3:00AM HUMAN TIME, EIGHT POUNDS, FOUR OUNCES. IN GOOD HEALTH. THE SPLICING OF GOMAI AND HUMAN CHROMOSOME 6/g6 SEEMS SUCCESSFUL. NO COMPLICATIONS THROUGHOUT GESTATION, AND NO FURTHER EVIDENCE OF REJECTION AFTER BIRTH. THE NONCODING ANOMOLY THAT PRESENTED ITSELF WITHIN THE THIRD TRIMESTER HAS DISAPPEARED AND HAS NOT AFFECTED IN ANY WAY THE BIRTH OR THE HEALTH OF THE CHILD. VERY PLEASED WITH THE RESULTS SO FAR, AND IF IN THREE MONTHS THERE ARE NO COMPLICATIONS OR ANY REEMERGENCE OF SAID ANOMALY THAT

WOULD REQUIRE TERMINATION OF SAID CHILD, WILL RECOMMEND THAT WE EXPAND THE PROGRAM TO INCLUDE OTHER WILLING FAMILIES. WILL RECOMMEND THAT WE INCREASE THE POPULATION OF THE FIRST WAVE OF SPECIAL CHILDREN TO TWELVE, AND THEN INCREASE EPONENTIALLY THEREAFTER ASSUMING ALL IS DEVELOPING PROPERLY.

Marie had asked that her sperm donor be anonymous, so as to shield the man from any legal and personal conflicts should the experiment be unsuccessful. She also wanted full authority to abort the child if the matter went south, and she did not want to fight it out in colony court should the father of the child assume the mantle of religious or moral intransigence. Michael Jace would be *her* child and hers alone. At the time, it seemed like a reasonable precaution.

But as the years ticked by, and everything seemed fine, he should have told her. Long wanted to tell her, but time kept slipping away. There was never any indication that Marie wanted to know. She was happy, and more importantly, their son Michael Jace, seemed happy. Why complicate matters further by adding a father?

Now here he stood, with six other anxious men and women of the colony, fully kitted out in enviro-suits, bearing carbines, and sweeping through the *Geneva* grassland for their missing children. Long had pleaded with Williams not to take weapons.

"Why antagonize the situation further?" he had argued. "They are children."

"Children who just killed their mothers," Williams replied.

"But they are still children. And our future. If they die, we die."

Williams had compromised and agreed to have all carbines set on safety, and promised to use force only if necessary. But 'if necessary' was a vague term. Long did not know to what lengths Williams would go to secure his murder suspects. And what would he do with them once they returned to the colony? There was no legal precedent for any of it.

A thin, rubbery polymer used on the colony ship for repairs had been smeared onto the enviro-suits, and that provided additional protection from *Geneva's* brutal bacterial and viral contagions. Perhaps as much as an additional twenty-four hours. It was hard to know for sure. In time, the polymer would peel off in the dry air like snake skin, and then they would not make it back to the colony without severe risk of exposure. They had a short window of opportunity to find their children, and the sun was setting.

"Perhaps we should stop and start a fire," Williams said. "They may come to us."

"What can we burn on this field?" Long asked.

Williams lowered his carbine, looked around. He shrugged. "The grass."

So they did. They spread out and pulled as much dry grass as they could find, piled it high, and set it alight. And like Earthen grass, it smoked.

The air was filled with a thick white-gray cloud that was carried across the sky, blotting out the sun, and making Long worry. They had burned *Geneva* grass before, but only around the habs, and only for a short while. This much smoke, so far away from their base, he wondered what would happen. Would it bring their children out from hiding, or would it bring down upon them the wrath of the Gomai? Long had never seen the species build fires; perhaps they didn't need them. What would they think of this now, their homeland being burned and violated? The Gomai were a docile species. Well, that was not always true, as he had discovered recently while investigating the murders…and the genetic anomaly that had appeared in Michael Jace's immune DNA during the third trimester.

They sat around the fire, their hands tight on their carbines. Long sweated in his enviro-suit, his eyes darted left and right to try to find movement in the grass. Everyone was quiet, everyone on edge.

Three hours later, they arrived.

First, it was the Gomai. A small group burst into the camp, on all fours, sniffing the air, the smoke, trying to figure it all out. Like marmosets, they darted in and out of the shadows, approaching the fire, pulling back, then huddling to discuss their findings. They were beautiful, Long had to admit. Their long necks, their elaborate patch-work of fur running down their spines gave them an ethereal quality in the shadow light that was quite arresting. This group did not wear clothing of any kind, though he remembered seeing some groups who did. Perhaps it was different by group. No one in the colony had bothered cataloguing Gomai behavioral patterns. They were too busy just trying to survive.

A deep whistle came out of the grass, beyond the light of the fire. The Gomai perked up then scattered.

The children emerged. Three at first, still wearing pajamas or other night clothing in which they had fled. Two girls and one boy who still had his dead mother's blood stains on his shirt. Then the rest, one after the other, until all twelve were inside the range of the fire ring. Long saw Michael Jace. Their eyes met. The boy spoke first.

"You are here to take us back?"

"We are," Williams said before Long could answer, reconfiguring his comm device so that his voice projected outside his suit. The officer stepped forward, gripping his carbine, though holding it low. Michael Jace neither moved nor spoke as William approached him.

"You all have killed seven mothers," Williams said. "*Your* mothers. You will come back, and you will explain why."

"Williams, please!" Long said, readjusting his comm as well, his patience growing short. "Let me speak."

The officer was about to object. Then he stepped aside and gave Long room to approach.

"I can fix this," Long said, laying his carbine down and stepping forward with hands raised in peace. "I know what happened."

"What do you mean?" Michael Jace asked.

"You were not supposed to exhibit any physical or mental signs of being Gomai. We were conducting simple immune chromosomal splices. But shortly before you were born, a genetic anomaly appeared in your code. It quickly disappeared, and it could not be rediscovered. So, we monitored your progress for the first few years on the assumption that it might reappear, but it never did. Not until you and Jenni and Chris and Sebastian and all of you began to express longer necks, patchy fur patterns, yellow eyes, and other Gomai physical traits. But it wasn't until you…killed your mothers that I fully understood."

"Understood what?" Michael Jace asked.

"That the Gomai had been, at one point, four separate species, each of which had immunity consistent with their region. But as their environment changed over thousands of years, individual groups were forced to travel longer distances to gather food and find shelter. This brought them into contact with other groups. Some were docile—like the Gomai are now—some were aggressive, and some were something in between. But unlike our Earth, the less aggressive species won out here, because the vast grassland required grazing, cooperation, and herding skills, not fighting skills. Everything that the Gomai needed nutritionally lived within this grass, and thus their more aggressive noncoding—junk DNA—fell dormant. I guess with the introduction of human DNA, those dormant strands have reactivated. But they don't function like normal DNA, taking up lines in your genome. Their sole purpose is to just appear and activate chemicals within your brain, chemicals that reactive behaviors and instincts of those species whose DNA did not survive. Do you understand?"

Michael Jace nodded. "We are smarter than you know, Milton Long." He raised his hands and motioned to the other children around him. "We look more human in your eyes than do the Gomai, but we understand this grass. We understand this land."

"Okay, then understand this: I can fix the problem. I cannot keep those dormant strands from reappearing, but I can change your brain chemistry to reject those signals. So, come back with us, and help us to make you better, so that you never do something like this again."

It seemed to Long that Michael Jace was thinking it through. The young boy stepped back a few paces, furrowed his brow, moved his long neck about like a snake sniffing the air. But then he said, "No, you do not understand. I did not kill my mother, Mayor Marie, because of dormant behaviors. I killed her because her blood is not in harmony with *Geneva*. It is not in harmony with the grass, or the rocks, or the water, or the sky. Your blood isn't in harmony either. Neither is yours, Officer Williams. None of you are in harmony with this land, and you never will be. So, please go back to your habs, and live out the rest of your days. We are not your children. We are Giraffa, and this is our home."

Williams stepped forward again. "That is not going to happen, young man. You have killed members of the colony, and you will have to answer for that. You will come with us willingly, or by force."

"Williams, please," Long tried to say, though by the time he had uttered the words, Michael Jace and another of the children were on Officer Williams, tearing the carbine from his hands and ripping a large gash in his enviro-suit.

In the heat of the moment, Long had not seen the other children move strategically so as to be two-on-one with the adult colonists. Like Michael had done to Williams, the other adults had their carbines ripped from their hands, and their suits compromised. The attack was so fast, so precise, that Long had no chance to respond, even if he wanted to. He stood there, mouth agape, too terrified, too amazed, to move.

When it was done, some of the humans tried to run off into the darkness, back toward the hab, as if they could make it in time. Williams tried to be aggressive and grabbed Michael by the throat, but the young boy just waited, enduring the pain, until Williams's breathing became labored, his lungs began to close in the hostile air. A few minutes later, he was dead, and Long knew that all of them would be in a very short time.

But not him. No one had touched him. He stood there, near the dying fire, surrounded by all the Giraffa children.

Michael Jace stepped up to him, as cool and as calm as Long had ever seen. "You may go, Milton Long. And tell them what I have said. You may live out your days, and we will live out ours, in *our* grass, in *our* home."

The children turned and disappeared, leaving Long there beside the fire. He tried to call out to Michael Jace, to tell him what he had meant to say, but the words caught in his throat. He said them to himself instead.

Michael Jace, you are my son, and I am your father.

Ten Years Later...

The last female colonist killed herself by stepping out of her hab and into the *Geneva* air. An hour later, Long pulled her back in and put her body in a bag for later cremation. But there would be no later this time, for she was the last. Only he remained. All the others were gone.

Year after year, he had gathered colonists' corpses from silly mistakes or suicide or from natural causes, had processed them, had given them last rights, and then turned on the flame. One after the other, until this day. In a way he was relieved. He had been waiting for this day. Now it was here.

After tagging her body, Long returned to his private hab. He climbed out of his enviro-suit, hung it up carefully, then put on a simple pair of tennis shoes and drab grey utilities. He then turned toward the airlock in his living quarters, took a deep breath, and then opened it.

The door burst out into the harsh *Geneva* air. He could breathe it, but not for long. That did not matter. He had planned this day for a long, long time.

He walked across the grass, in the direction where he and Williams and the others had gone to confront the children. He walked twenty paces, and then the heaviness of the air overwhelmed him and he collapsed.

Hands were on him immediately, pulling him upright. He coughed, opened his eyes. Michael Jace was there.

He was older, an adult now. His neck had grown longer. He had never grown those impressive fur patches that other Giraffa had, but he was still impressive. Tall. Sturdy. Lovely.

"I am glad to see you again, Michael Jace," Long said, his eyes beginning to tear, both from emotion and from the bacteria swirling around in the air. "I was worried you would not come."

"I have been waiting for this day for a long time, Father. Just as long as you have."

Long's heart skipped. "You knew? All this time?"

Michael Jace nodded. "I have always known. And I wanted to take this moment to show you your grandchildren."

Two little Giraffa came up to him, a girl, a boy, leery, uncertain. Long looked down at them and smiled. They had their father's eyes. The girl's neck was shorter than her brother's. She had fur patches. He did not. They were lovely.

"I am ready to die."

"Not yet, Father. Come."

He was led further into the grass, hundreds of feet from the hab, and down a small hillock. Then before him, rising out of the grass like a tree, he saw it.

It was a monument of grass, woven tightly together like an old Earthen basket. Strong, sturdy. It had a place for him to lie down, and behind that platform, Long could see the modest shape of a person, a human, weaved out of red and deep green grass, like a sculpture.

"What…what is this?"

"It is for you, Father," Michael Jace said, leading Long to the platform and helping him lie down. "You are not just my father. You are *all* of our fathers. You made us who we are, and you will pass in honor."

Long did not hold back his tears any longer. With assistance, he lay down, letting the Geneva air choke him as he tried speaking once more.

"I need to tell you something, Michael, my — my son. More are coming. More humans. Hundreds. Thousands. Maybe tens of thousands. There will be more humans than you can handle."

"Their blood will not be in harmony either."

"It won't matter. There will be too — too many of them for you to defeat. They will k — kill you all."

Michael Jace gripped Long's hand, and smiled. He had his mother's smile. "Have faith in your creation, Father. Have faith in your children."

Long raised his head. Giraffa children stood around him, by the hundreds, perhaps thousands. Farther than he could see. In unison, they raised their hands, stretched their long necks, and whistled into the air. He did not know what they were saying, but that did not matter. They were there for him, and he was grateful.

Milton Long laid his head down, closed his eyes, and fell into harmony.

GOOD ADVICE

John L. French

"LOOK OUT! IT'S A MONSTER! KILL IT!"

The cry came from a young boy in the crowd gathered to witness the arrival of the Anansi on Earth. It was, perhaps, not the best greeting for visitors to Earth to receive, but it was understandable.

The Anansi were not the first extra-Terran race humanity had encountered but none of the others had looked so—alien. The rest had all conformed to the basic model—a head atop an upright torso, two arms, two legs. There were of course variations in skin color and texture, and some had senses that worked in ways different than ours, but they looked…human, or at least humanoid.

Not so the Anansi. Their appearance tapped into an atavistic fear that is buried in quite a few humans.

They were creatures of the dark.

They were the stuff of our nightmares.

They were spiders.

Spiders the size of ponies.

At least they looked like spiders. Two body segments joined by a flexible cylinder that allowed them to raise their thorax roughly ninety degrees from their rear abdomen. Six legs on the latter for locomotion while the thorax bore the remaining pair which were used as "arms." Their heads seemed smaller than they should and were featureless except for a mouth and two round discs that served for sensory input.

Three of them had descended from their crude, yet functional ship to be greeted by the Secretary General of Earth United. One was black, another a medium brown, and the last bore the coloration of Australia's dreaded red-backed spider.

The boy's outcry had come at just as the Secretary General was to speak. As the boy was at the front of the crowd, it was heard by everyone, including Earth's newest guests. As the SG stood there wondering just what to say or do, from the brown Anansi came the twittering, clicking, and chirping that was their natural language. What was conveyed by the language app of our IMplants and over the loud speaker was:

simulated chuckling. <funny, that is exactly what one of our crew members said about your race.> more simulated chuckling.

This was followed by a certain twist of its head that we would later learn served as their smile.

Who knew that an alien race would have such a gracious sense of humor?

After that, meetings and negotiations went smoothly. The Anansi were new to space travel and humanity was only the second extra-system race they had encountered. It was agreed that each would establish a delegation on the other's world to explore how each could benefit the other.

I should explain that "Anansi" is not their word for themselves. The term by which they refer to themselves translates as "human." When "Anansi" was suggested it was quickly adopted. When our guests were told of this and the myths and legends behind the name they seemed quite flattered.

The Anansi legation set up their ship in the Dominican Rain Forest, saying that it reminded them of their home planet. Earth's legation was carefully selected (no arachnophobes allowed) and set out in an EU ship accompanied by the black Anansi whom everyone jointly dubbed "Charlotte." When told of the derivation of this name it chuckled and chirped in apparent approval.

Two years later not much progress had been made. Neither side benefited much by the other's space-travel technology. Neither side knew how to send messages through space faster than light. We learned about their planet and natural resources and they learned about ours. Trade items were identified and mutually beneficial agreements were reached. Life on Earth went on much the same as it always had, the realization that "we were not alone" not having changed things all that much.

Which is why two years and three days after the Anansi landed on Earth I was put on a shuttle flight from Canaveral to the Earth-Luna Lagrange Station and from there on to a FTL ship bound for the Anansi system.

I'm a cop, and there had been a murder. The first ever on an extra-solar planet.

As I said, nothing had changed all that much.

My name is Abel Cooper. I'm an at-large detective for Earth United's Investigative Service. We get called in if something happens that involves more than one country or might have global implications.

The case I had just finished was nothing out of the ordinary. A team of jewel thieves moving from one country to another thinking that would keep them a few steps ahead of justice. Their plan worked, for the first two crimes. By the time they'd committed their third we were on to them and before they committed their fourth we had them locked up in a Sao Paulo jail.

Which meant that I was available when the message ship arrived from Anansi. The Terran legation of 30 people was now down to 29, the death of number 30 being described as "suspicious in nature." Based on the accompanying files and scans this was diplomat speak for "Jame Lancaster was stabbed three times in the chest and no one's confessed to killing her yet."

Off-planet legations do not travel with investigators, security teams, or anything else that might lead our alien friends to conclude that we do not trust them. We don't, of course, and are probably right in not doing so. Just as they would be right not to trust us. It is, I'm told, the only way that diplomacy works, on this or any world.

Having been given the assignment, I packed for a three-week trip. A week's trip through the Ackley Field to Anansi and another week for the return. According to the file, the murder weapon had been found — a knife that was still in the third stab wound. A DNA and fingerprint scan should reveal who had wielded it and if not, a Marston cord would sort through any lies I was told. I figured three days for the investigation followed by a few days of R&R on another planet.

The FTL was AI-piloted. With nothing else to do I read, watched vids, and caught up on the sleep I missed during my last case. I also spent part of the outbound week reading the files on the legation and in a VR review of the crime scene. Bloodstain patterns gave me an estimate of where the killer had been standing and how tall he or she might be. There was also an excellent chance that the killer had gotten blood on his or her clothing. Something else to scan for. My job was getting easier and easier. It was looking like even with R&R I'd be inbound within twenty days, perhaps even less.

When the ship touched down at the Anansi spaceport I was greeted by what had become their traditional greeting for Terrans.

<look out! it's a monster! kill it!>

I played along, turning around and around as if looking for the creature before "suddenly realizing" the speaker was referring to me.

I smiled. It tilted its head and we were friends and comrades.

My new best buddy was a medium-sized, black-and-red Anansi whom someone dubbed "Parker." At least that's how it introduced itself. It then went on to explain that it would be serving as my host and guide as well as "assisting" me in my investigation into the death of Jame Lancaster.

<have never seen Terran death practices.> it clicked, whistled, and chirped. *<my government is/I am interested in your procedures.>*

I could have refused. But my orders had been to "cooperate fully" with our eight–legged friends and I did not want to be the first to create an interplanetary incident.

What could it hurt? Showing swift and sure justice could only help our standing with them.

Or so I thought.

My arrival at the Terran legation was met with less than enthusiasm. No surprise there. I was the outsider. I was the law. I was the guy who was going to take one of them back for a quick trial and a lengthy imprisonment. And who knew what else I might find in my snooping around.

Tory Morales was the only one who met me. He was the chief legate. He had the look of the professional bureaucrat who knew that a posting parsecs from Earth was likely as high he was going to rise in the Diplomatic Corp. When and if an embassy was established the ambassadorship would go either to a political ally or enemy, depending on how valuable the Anansi might prove to be in the future.

"Mr. Morales."

"Detective Cooper."

As he took my hand I gave him the possible-suspect once over — left-handed (the killer was likely a righty) and taller than my estimate. I moved him to the bottom of my list.

I introduced my new best friend. "This is Parker, who, at the request of his government, will be 'assisting' me with my investigation."

The look Morales gave me spoke more than he could safely say in front of Parker. It also told me that once out of earshot (or whatever the spiders used to hear with) we would have a more meaningful — and vocal — conversation.

"I'll need to speak with the rest of the legation. How many are currently present?'

"All the ones that were here at the time of Jame's death, Detective. Myself, Juliet Sharp, Alex Burch, Yolanda Santiago, and Granville Head. Sharp's our medical officer. The rest of the legation is scattered around the planet, doing surveys, taking tours, and looking for ways to enrich the cultural exchange between our two worlds."

More diplo-speech for looking for something, anything that the spiders had that we didn't but needed. Then would come the job of convincing them that they desperately needed something we had but didn't want.

"I'll examine the scene and the weapon tomorrow morning," I told Morales. "Once that's done I'll interview the staff. It shouldn't take me more than a few days to finish up."

And start my R&R, I mentally added, wondering…no, hoping that there would be at least one of the staff would be attractive, female, innocent, and willing to R&R with me.

"In the meantime, Mr. Morales, there are questions I need to ask about the progress your legation is making."

I turned to Parker, who had been standing silently by my side the whole time. "If you will excuse Mr. Morales and me for the evening — Earth business, you understand."

<certainly, friend cooper. secrets, confidences, private talk. you will wait tomorrow for my return before proceeding?>

After I assured it that I would, it scuttled off to wherever the Anansi go when they're not watching us "four-limbs." (Their name for us, as I understand it.)

It was just Morales and me for dinner.

"You'll have to excuse my staff. There's been a lack of sociability since Jame's death. It's…difficult having one of your co-workers killed and knowing that another one did it. Four of us suspecting the rest while the fifth one waits it out. I think whoever it is would have long since fled if there was anywhere to go."

"I should have the answer soon, Mr. Morales. In the meantime I have questions of another sort."

He gave me a rueful look. "Let me guess - How are things going? Have you made any progress? What have you learned about the Anansi?" He paused then asked, "Did I leave anything out?"

"You hit the basics."

"As well as can be expected. Not much. Damn little." Morales shook his head. "This is the ass end of nowhere. There's nothing on this planet that Earth doesn't have, expect giant spiders and other plants and animals that would excite an exobiologist but no one else. As for progress—again, there's nothing major they have that we want, which means who the hell cares if they need something of ours."

"What about the Anansi themselves. What have you learned?"

"They live in small social groups. Those groups form larger groups and so on. There's some industry. They only make what they need."

"And they needed a spaceship?'

Another head shake. "They got that from the Karp in exchange for mining rights to their moon." Before I could ask, he added, "Nothing on that we need either."

Then I asked the question everyone on Earth was wondering since the Anansi landed.

"Have you learned anything about their, um, social interactions?"

That got a chuckle from my host. "If you meaning screwing, say so. As far as we know, they don't. They were surprised to learn how humans do it. They actually asked to witness our 'reproductive procedures.'"

"And?"

Morales smiled. "Two of our more exhibitionist delegates were happy to comply. But our hosts have not responded in kind. When asked all they've said was 'We eat. We die.' Maybe they exchange DNA through cannibalism."

Just then something fast, furry, and about the size of a Chihuahua skittered across the room.

"What the hell was that?"

When Morales stopped laughing he explained. "We call them rugrats. They're everywhere on this planet, like roaches in Manhattan, lizards in Florida, or monkeys in Costa Rica. If you're here long enough you'll get used to them."

I didn't plan on being here that long. "Anything else about the spiders?"

"Only that they're the most boring sentients we've run across. No culture at all—no literature, no plays, no music. They only thing we seem to have in common is humor. They enjoy wordplay and love slapstick and practical jokes."

Morales and I left it there. I went up to my room, had a good night's sleep, and woke up ready to catch a killer.

The next morning, at seven Terran time, Parker was waiting outside the legation for me.

"It's been there all morning," said someone who introduced himself as Granville Head.

"Invite it in for breakfast," I said.

Parker declined pancakes but did enjoy syrup-covered bacon.

Once we'd cleaned up, Parker taking longer than me, we went to the scene of the crime. In this case Lancaster's bedroom. Her body had been removed, but what blood had been spilled and spattered was still there.

Parker watched in silence as I mentally compared the actual scene with my memory of the virtual one. When I started taking samples it said,

<our fluid is green>

It made no other comment as I scanned the rumpled bedclothes and took additional samples when I got a positive indication.

The next stop was the health clinic, part of which was designed to serve as a morgue should a legate die. Lancaster's body was there, preserved in stasis. The knife that had killed her was on a separate table in its own protective field. It was a steak knife. I had seen several like it last night in the kitchen.

Doctor Sharp seemed somewhat uncomfortable with Parker in the room, but that was her problem and not mine. As before, the Anansi stayed silent while I worked.

"Did you do an autopsy?"

Sharp nodded. "An internal scan. Three stabs wounds, two in the left lung, the last in the heart. Cause of death, the one in the heart."

"Who removed the knife?"

"I did, wearing gloves. I put it right into stasis. Tory and Alex witnessed my doing so."

"Release the field."

When Sharp complied I picked up the murder weapon. Blood on the blade near the tip. A slightly visible print near the guard. Nothing visible on the handle. I scanned the print and swabbed the rest.

Returning to my room, I set up my instruments and started them working. In a few minutes they'd finish their analysis and started comparisons with known samples of the legates' DNA and fingerprints. That should tell me who. Then all I'd need was the why.

As my instruments worked, I turned to my eight-legged shadow.

"Do you have any questions?"

It did, and I explained about DNA and fingerprints. The Anansi had the former, but the digits on their forelimbs exuded a light adhesive with which to grip objects rather than friction ridges.

<*the dead one. how did death happen?*>

"She was stabbed in the heart."

<*stabbed?*> Parker asked, twisting its head in a way I later learned meant puzzlement.

"Yes, stabbed. Someone used the knife you saw me examine and stabbed her three times."

<*someone. one of your kind caused the death of another? why would this be?*>

"As soon as I know who it was I hope to have the answer myself."

Parker made no comment to this. In fact, it went rigid, not moving for a minute or two. Just as I was worried that it was sick or something, it said,

<*thank you friend cooper. must go now.*>

I escorted it to the door and watched it leave. Not the first of my mistakes that evening.

By the time I got back to my room the instruments had done their work. Parker slipped out of my mind as I read the results. It was time for the big meeting.

I met the five legation members in the common room and got right to it.

"Burch, Head—the two of you were involved with Jame Lancaster." I used my cop voice, the one that knew everything, the one that didn't allow for doubt or contradiction. "Three DNA profiles on the bed. Hers and both of yours. Burch, your DNA on the knife handle, hers on the blade. Your thumb print on the blade. Jealousy, not the oldest motive ever, but close to it. Really, didn't your mother teach you to share?"

Burch didn't try to deny it. "What's going to happen to me?"

I shrugged. "I don't know. You'll go back with me on the FTL. You'll find out then. Try coming up with an argument for manslaughter because your use of the kitchen knife makes it look like Murder One."

The door chime rang just as I was telling Burch to confine himself to his room. Morales excused himself. As I was warning the others not to take any action on their own he came back.

"Cooper, you're needed. The rest of you…" He tried to finish the sentence. He couldn't. Maybe he whispered "pray" as he led me to the entrance.

"What is it?" I asked.

"It's…bad."

Standing just outside the door was Parker. Next to it was a larger, brown Anansi.

"Shelob," Morales whispered to me. "The head of the local group."

Behind those two were more spiders than I had even imagined. More than enough to surround the legation. Enough to do whatever they wanted.

<your species kills its own.>

This from the one called Shelob.

There was no denying this. I had admitted as much to Parker. My first mistake, although I hadn't realized it at the time. My second was letting it leave.

"Yes, we do," I said simply and firmly.

<you would do the same to us.>

Eventually, I thought. *If you have something we wanted badly enough.* Morales gave some sort of weak denial. Shelob did not believe him.

<the one you termed Charlotte has taken your ship. it will go in your place to Earth. there — condolences for the tragedy that killed you all.>

Even if the legation had any weapons other than kitchen knives I doubted that we could mount any kind of defense against so many. Besides, I was police, not military, so I did what any cop would do, I dumped the problem on the guy in charge.

"You're the diplomat, Morales. Do something."

<we will recompense for your loss. Anansi food called…>

There was a moment before the software could translate. When it did it came out as "rugrat."

<Terrans will enjoy. will not resist. many will eat. will have to eat. before long they will die.>

With no further explanation we were forced back into the house and not allowed out until the FLT had departed. Apparently our "tragic deaths" was a lie that Charlotte would tell when it landed.

It wasn't until that evening that I figured it out.

"We eat, we die," Not cannibalism. Like their Earth counterparts the Anansi devour their mates. Their DNA combines and the young burst forth, killing both mother and father.

Parker confirmed part of this.

"Why," I asked it, "if the Anansi are so opposed to murder?"

<you are not our species. it is not what you call murder. it is defending ourselves.>

Sharp, after catching a few of the rugrats and doing a necropsy, confirmed the rest.

"It's viral DNA of a sort. It turns certain cells into zygotes. These cells start to divide and the wonderful process of creation begins. At least for Anansi. Humans will probably just die horribly as they burst apart."

"Unless the virus finds a way to combine with human DNA," offered Head. "I wonder who the children will take after."

"It doesn't matter," Morales said. "The Anansi didn't take the time to think this through. They didn't know what murder was until we taught them." Here he cut a glance toward me, as if I was to blame. Maybe I was. "And now they've attacked a species that has no compunctions against killing its own, much less monsters out of people's nightmares. I only hope the other races stay out of the war that's coming."

Look out! It's a monster! Kill it!

That young boy had good advice. I only hope the other alien races don't look our way and take it.

LUCKY STRIKE

Christopher M. Hiles

Day 0
0730 Hours

Pudge floated in front of the sensor station that showed the pixelated image of a large asteroid. He was the first person brought out of cold sleep by the computer. He was, also, the first to be able to look at the asteroid, albeit using an impressive set of telescopes. The asteroid was making a beeline toward humanity's first colony. To the colony, the asteroid was an extinction-level event. To Pudge, it was just asteroid NC-190275-C. Pudge grunted and shifted the toothpick that seemed to be a permanent feature to the other side of his mouth.

"What are we looking at?" asked the ship's captain and owner, Danny Mierdah, who floated in to the compartment and stopped next to Pudge. When Pudge didn't reply, he nudged Pudge and repeated his question.

Pudge flinched. "Jesus, Skipper, you scared the shit out of me!"

"Not literally, right?"

"I'd imagine you'd know if it was…"

"So, is that maximum magnification?"

Pudge nodded. "Yeah. We're about a two days. The computer has already put us on an intercept course with it."

"It's big," the captain said.

"Yup," Pudge said. "We might get a bit more money than we thought."

"Oh?" the captain said.

"It's about 5% bigger than originally calculated," Pudge said. "I have no idea how the hell the scans missed this when they scanned the area."

"Well, that was nearly a century ago."

"No excuse for piss-poor planning."

"You know I can't argue with that," the captain said and looked at Pudge. "I know you're an expert and all, but I think even the likes of you may have missed something…"

"Yeah, what's that?"

"You have failed to put a stitch of clothes on."

"I was getting around to it," Pudge said and pushed himself toward his quarters.

Danny heard the familiar sounds of a crew getting their first meal after a year's worth of cold sleep. It was a chorus of groans and slurping of food out of pouches. The kitchen was the largest area on the ship. It served as a dining area, a meeting space, an entertainment area, and an emergency shelter.

Danny pushed off the wall to place himself in the middle of the pie-shaped room. He reached up and grabbed a small handhold to settle himself.

"Good morning, everyone!" he said, as bright and cheerfully as he could muster. The crew booed and a couple of the most salty members chucked empty food packs at him. This expression of appreciation had gone from a one-time incident many years ago to a full-on tradition. Per the custom, Danny acted upset. "Whoever threw that had better clean it up or I will toss him or her out the airlock!

"Alright," he said. "Welcome aboard the *Lucky Strike* on its twenty-second mining job. I know that you are usually briefed on the details prior to entering the big sleep; but, the powers that be wanted to keep this operation under wraps." The crew straightened up and was now giving him their undivided attention. "We are almost at our destination, asteroid NC-190275-C. It was discovered by an asteroid-mapping probe about a month before we left. It's a big one and it will impact the colony in 11 months and that's why they wanted to keep it secret. Should it impact, it will obliterate the colony and anything else living on the surface.

"Our job is to make sure that the asteroid doesn't hit and still turn a profit. We're going to do what we always do: find a soft spot, put a rock thrower on the surface, and set it to ejecting rocks into our net. In the process, it should alter the asteroids off course just enough to miss the planet.

"In case there isn't a soft spot, we will make one. Per usual, the Commonwealth Navy has provided us with one shape-charged nuclear warhead and three of its finest to handle it. You all know Chief Fuller and Petty Officer Chao from previous hops. The new member of the team is Lieutenant Sanchez. She's new to us and to Civil Support, so everyone play nice." The group mumbled a welcome as Sanchez smiled and nodded.

"Our ETA is two days," Danny continued. "Pudge will launch our seeker drones tomorrow once we're in range. After we receive their telemetry, our astrogeologists will identify the best possible location to fire our ejecta disks so we can place the thrower.

"I have opened up communications so you can send messages to your families letting them know you're awake, alive, and living the dream. Do *not* discuss the mission outside of anything you'd say on a routine mission. The computer will freeze any message that breaks this rule.

"Finally, and on a lighter note, this is Pudge's last mission as he's just completed his 80th extended sleep. As you know, anyone attempting more than 80 sleeps begins to lose their faculties. I'm not sure Pudge ever had control over his to begin with… In any case, I think he's due for a new call sign. Since he's getting up there in age, I put to the group that we go with 'Gramps'. What say you?"

A tall man floating near the wall shouted above the den, "How the hell old are you, Pudge?"

"Not counting cold sleep, I'm 41," Pudge replied while staring at Danny.

"Uh-huh, and *with* cold sleep?" the man asked.

Pudge groaned and said, "I'm somewhere north of 84."

This got the group shouting names including Ancient One, Captain Decrepit, NAW (which stood for Needs a Walker), and Mummy. However, the name that seemed to annoy Pudge the most was Gramps and that, of course, was the name he was given.

"Gramps it is, then!" Danny said.

"I think there may be a return of the phantom shitter," Gramps said. "100 credits to anybody who gets the phantom shitter to come out of retirement."

"If I find a turd in my sack, you're going to have to sleep in it!" Danny said. "Alright, that being said, get settled in, first watch starts at 1200 ship-board."

Day One
0900 Hours

Gramps was manning the seeker drone station. The ship had sent out a set of four drones to circle the asteroid, taking readings that would help guide the crew to the best spots to begin the mining process. It helped eliminate surprises, something you never want when you're a year away from the nearest colony.

He locked the ship's sensors on to the asteroid and the computer gave him a set time to launch the drones. Launching them closer in wasn't a problem but they had a very limited range. They were able to maneuver within tolerances that would turn a human into a flat hamburger patty.

Danny floated up next to Gramps. "How long 'til we can launch 'em?"

"A couple of hours. They'll arrive tonight and then we'll have a much better idea of what we're facing."

"Frankly, I hope it's a soft one. I know that means less of a payday but it'll be that much easier to neutralize it as a threat."

"Yeah, but it's a kilometer long and three quarters of that in width. Even if it is a soft one, it's still a long potato. We're still pretty far out for our sensor suite but we haven't seen any evidence of a debris field being dragged behind it."

"Doesn't bode well for an easy target."

"Don't give up hope, Skipper," Gramps said turning to look at Danny. "You look like shit. Didn't you sleep well last night?"

"Let's just say that either you owe several people 100 credits or one person had a big dinner before they went to sleep. I had to get a backup bag and dispose of my old one."

"The phantom shitter works in mysterious ways," Gramps said with a smile.

"You're lucky you're so old. It wouldn't look good for the skipper to beat up an old man."

1830 Hours

Gramps floated next to the drone station with a couple of scientists peering over his shoulder. He pushed a button on one of the communication pads, "Skipper to the Con, please."

"I'm already here," Danny said as he floated through the access hatch. "What's up?"

"We've lost contact with two of our drones," Gramps replied.

"What do you mean 'lost contact'?"

"Just that. All four drones entered orbit around the 'roid and began their sweep. About two minutes after that, drones one and four shut down. Not getting any signal from either of 'em. I've given drone three orders to scan for drone one with a four kilometer standoff distance so we don't lose it, too."

"Shit," Danny said. "How long before we arrive?"

"Forty-five hours," Gramps replied.

"Alright, let me know what you find. I'm going to talk to engineering and see if either were recently worked on by maintenance."

"Aye, aye," Gramps said.

Danny pushed himself through the access port and down the main spine of the ship, running fore and aft. Near the rear end, he took a down tube and emerged in the engineering bay. The Chief Engineer was working through a checklist with his assistants.

"Chao," Danny said.

Chao was a short man with a rim of black hair around his head. At the moment, he was stuck in an access tube. Danny heard a clank and a muffled curse before Chao emerged, rubbing his head. He composed himself and said, "Skipper?"

"We lost contact with two of our drones," Danny said. "I need you to check the maintenance logs and see if there were any issues before we launched and who did the final check-offs."

"Yes, sir," Chao replied. "I'm the one who did the prelaunch checks. All the drones were in perfect working order." He pulled up the maintenance logs on a display panel built into the wall. He skimmed through the records and shook his head. "Nothing here, either, boss. Drone one is brand new and drone four was on our last cruise, but we didn't use it."

"Are you sure?"

"Yes, sir," Chao said as he skimmed the last operations completed before the drones went dead. His face contorted into a mask of confusion. "That's odd."

"What's odd?"

"The last command given to both the drones was a cold shutdown order. *We* shut them down."

"That's not possible. Gramps has been watching them since they entered orbit around the asteroid."

"The order came from his terminal," Chao said moving aside to let Danny move in.

"That doesn't make sense," Danny said as he scratched his head. "Why would the terminal have sent a cold shutdown order if it wasn't detecting any immediate danger?"

"I'll run diagnostics and see what prompted it to send that order but I'd advise using an auxiliary station until we know for sure."

"I'll have him move. Let me know as soon as you have something."

When Danny reached the Con, he shooed them off of the panel and to the next one. "Engineering is going to pull that console apart in a few." The small group parted to let Danny squeeze in with them.

"Talk to me, Gramps," he said.

"I've got 'em booted back up and they are restarting their original missions. I have no idea how the shutdown code was sent. These guys can vouch for me on that," Gramps said motioning to the scientists, who both nodded.

"I trust you. We just have a very limited timeframe and a narrow margin of error. Keep me updated."

Day 2
0700 Hours

Danny always had a hard time falling asleep the night before a major maneuver. Considering the weight of the situation and the error with the drones, sleep was more elusive than ever. Luckily, the scientists seemed to have the same problem and gave him their report around midnight.

His first letdown was that some areas of the asteroid were denser than he'd ever seen before. The drones picked up a magnetic field close to the surface, leading the science team to believe that parts of the asteroid were made out of ferrous metals. They couldn't tell exactly which metals, probably iron or cobalt. He could turn a good profit on the job but it was going to make it more difficult to dig in and push the asteroid off its course. He sighed and hoped that the ejecta tests would show a chink in the surface where a fusion bomb could open a crack in its armor.

Danny slipped out of his sleeping sack, washed up, and got dressed. He wore his customary coveralls in addition to a harness that would help his body fight against the g-forces that came with a hard maneuver. Each crewmember had one and it was fitted to their specific needs. A lot of people complained that they were uncomfortable, but Danny had been using his for over 20 years and it felt fine to him.

Danny slid open the door to his sleep closet and made his way to the Con. Gramps was sitting at the navigation station and one of the scientists was chatting with Lieutenant Sanchez. He gave each of them a nod and said, "Good morning."

He floated over to Gramps. "How's it?"

"Another morning in paradise, Skipper," Gramps said.

"Are we going to have any problems today?"

"If we do, it'll be a surprise to both of us. The course is laid into the computer and we're going to take a nice and gentle bank to port until we're next to the asteroid with it on our starboard side. I've set it so that we'll be fifty kilometers away, just in case."

"When do we start?"

"Ninety-four minutes, twenty-eight seconds," Gramps said.

"Start the clock," Danny said.

"Yup," Gramps said and, a few seconds later, an alert sounded throughout the ship warning the small crew to strap in or else go for a wild ride.

"It being your last hop, I'm surprised you haven't asked to do this on manual."

"Well, Skipper, I figured that I should wait for you to bring it up." After a pause, Gramps looked up at Danny. "So, can I?"

"All yours. Try not to hit that big rock out there."

"Skipper?" Chao called from the entry coaming.

"Duty calls," Danny said. He pushed himself off of the deck and toward Chao softly landing in front of him. "What have you got?"

Chao held up the drone control console. "I replaced the console just in case, boss, but I can't find any faults with it. The signal definitely came from this console."

Danny exhaled, "You're absolutely sure?"

Chao nodded. "Absolutely."

Danny glanced over his shoulder at Gramps. "Alright, stow the console and keep an eye on what Gramps is doing, but be quiet about it."

"You got it, boss," Chao said. "One more thing," he hesitantly said.

"Great," Danny said. "Hit me."

"Someone outside of the ship has been accessing our main computer."

"Someone?"

"The records don't show who it was. I assume they were tampered with or deleted."

"Is it related to our control issues?"

"I wouldn't think so, skipper. It seems the only things they retrieved were the dictionary and editing software."

Danny shook his head, "Just… just make sure it isn't related."

"Yes, sir," Chao said before pushing himself up the access tube and towards Engineering.

Danny floated back into Ops and took his seat. After a few moments, he felt someone was staring at him. He turned and saw it was Sanchez. Danny held his gaze until she looked away. "Shit," Danny muttered.

"Two minutes until interface," Gramps said.

Danny had locked himself into his chair. He felt the squeeze of his g-suit as its tubes connected to the chair's fluid reservoir. He pulled his panel out of its pocket in the chair and locked it into place just above his left armrest. The screen showed him a diagram of the ship with icons for each crewmember. Several were green, indicating they were locked in and ready. A few remained red.

He tapped on the overhead communication button. "Get your asses locked in. Gramps is doing this manually so it'll probably be a bumpy ride!"

Gramps looked over his shoulder. "Thanks, Skipper… sixty seconds to interface. There will be three burns lasting 30 seconds each with a 10 second break in between. We'll be pulling 12 g's at most."

Though the chairs were rated for 15 g's, they didn't make the ride comfortable. It couldn't be helped, though. Turning a ship as large as the *Lucky Strike* required a lot of energy. The computer at the navigation station could do this automatically. Some pilots and captains trusted it. Others barely trusted it when all it was doing is keeping the ship going straight.

Danny looked down at his panel and saw that every crew member was finally locked down. A button at the top of the console glowed green. Danny pressed it, signaling Gramps to begin the maneuver when he was ready. "Everyone's strapped down, Gramps."

"Roger that," Gramps said. "Fifteen seconds to interface."

Danny tried to relax his body. The chair and his g-suit would do most of the work. He checked his straps one final time and then heard Gramps shout "ignition!" Danny was immediately shoved back into his seat.

Danny struggled to bring up the readout for their planned trajectory and their actual. Even with the ship jostling under the acceleration, Gramps was flying the ship perfectly.

"Standby for 10 second shutoff," Gramps said. "Remember, only 10 seconds!"

Danny felt the ship give one last shake before the g-forces melted away. He checked the crew's status and everyone was still locked in. Again, he pressed the green button giving Gramps control.

"Three seconds," Gramps said.

Three seconds later, the ship's engines fired back up and began the turn to put the ship next to the asteroid. The final burn would be used to make small corrections and provide retro thrust to match the asteroid's speed.

Danny brought up the navigation screen. Gramps was flying the ship perfectly. "Five seconds," Gramps said.

Five seconds came and went. The ship's engines continued to burn. The navigation screen showed that the ship was about to leave the target area. Five more seconds came and went.

"Gramps?" Danny said.

"I'm not doing this. If I hit the shut-off button any harder, my finger will go through the fucking screen!"

The ship's engines spit out more thrust. The deck began to rattle and an alarm went off followed by a calm, female voice.

"Warning, thrust reaching 100% of tolerance," the computer said.

"I'm fighting the controls!" Gramps said.

"Shit," Danny muttered. "Engineering!"

"According to my panel, Gramps' shut-off button should be working," Chao said.

"Warning, thrust is at 105% of tolerance. G-forces will exceed safe levels in 20 seconds," the computer reported.

"Try cutting it again, Gramps!" Danny shouted.

Danny could see Gramps simultaneously trying to keep the ship within the acceptable window while pressing the shutdown button. Gramps' hand slammed the button and the engines shut down.

Sweat ran down Danny's face. He wiped it away and took a deep breath. "Engineering, figure out what's wrong with my ship. Gramps, I'm showing that we are close to the boundary putting us 150 kilometers away from the asteroid. Is that what you're station is showing?"

"Yeah, Skipper," Gramps replied. He turned to face Danny. "It wasn't me. It was like the ship had a mind of its own!"

"I believe you," Danny said. "Let's focus on slowing us down."

The ship was traveling seventy-five kilometers a second faster than the asteroid, well within the ship's retro system ability to still match their speeds. It would burn more fuel which meant a smaller payout for the crew.

"I'm not seeing anything at the moment," Chao said over the private channel between him and Danny.

"I want you to fire the retros and get us back on track," Danny said. Gramps looked crestfallen. Danny mouthed the word "sorry". Gramps turned back to his panel.

"We're going to fire retros in 10 seconds and will burn for 27 seconds," Chao said.

"Copy, 10 seconds," Danny said. He looked at his panel, saw everyone was where they were supposed to be, and pressed the green button freeing Chao to activate the thrusters.

There was no need to announce when the thrusters were lit. Danny was thrown into his straps as the ship slowed down. The ship shook as it was forced to decelerate. It was the worst Danny had experienced in a long time. Right before he felt he couldn't take it anymore, Chao shouted *"shutdown!"* into his headset and the thrusters stopped.

"Gramps, position?" Danny said.

"We are 124 kilometers out and we've matched the speed of the asteroid."

"Great," Danny said. "Chao, please sound the ship."

"Roger," Chao said.

"Gramps, report to the medical bay."

Gramps sadly nodded, unbuckled from his station, and floated out the access port. Danny looked at Lieutenant Sanchez, who was staring back at him. Danny locked his gaze for a few moments and then turned to the science station. "Prepare the railgun and let me know when you're ready to fire."

"On it, boss," one of the scientists said.

Danny hit the all-call button. "All stations, we've completed our maneuvering. You're free to move."

Danny unlocked his harness and floated through the access port to his quarters. They were the size of a telephone booth with the majority of the space dedicated to housing his sleeping bag. He pulled out a computer pad that he used to access to the official ship's log. As much as he didn't want to write an incident report on Gramps, he knew that there would be a medical record as well as navigation data showing a manual change to the flight plan. Besides, it was the right thing to do.

Danny felt a slight breeze on the back of his neck. "How can I help you?"

"I was about to ask you the same thing," Sanchez said.

"I don't think so," Danny said as he turned around. "Do you need anything from me for your incident report?"

Sanchez looked confused. "Incident report?"

"Yeah, from the navigation error."

"My nuke is secure. How you fly your ship is your business," she said with a smile and what Danny swore was a twinkle in her brown eyes.

"Think you could fly it better?" Danny asked.

"I'm a fighter jock. I'm the best pilot I know!" she replied.

"I should have figured," Danny said. "Takes one to know one."

"You were a fighter jock? Who'd you fly with?"

"305th based out of Europa Station," Danny replied.

"Damn good squadron… damn shame what they did to it," Sanchez said looking down at her boots.

"There wasn't anyone left to fight," Danny said. "Anyway, I learned a lot about taking care of your wingman."

"Was Gramps a fighter pilot? He seemed to want to fly the *Lucky Strike* like it was one."

"No, just an old friend."

"Hmmm," Sanchez said. "Well, I suppose the question is whether or not you're really helping him by letting him continue to sit in the pilot's seat."

"We've only got one more maneuver to do. The rest will be drone-based and the science folks manage that; and, of course, you if we need to make it glow."

"Speaking of," Sanchez said pulling a small pad out of her suit's pocket. "Chief asked me to give you this. It's his preliminary assessment of where we're going to have to place the nuke."

"He's done this every trip with just the telemetry from the probes. He's only been wrong once. I think he took that as an insult."

"The Chief Petty Officer is a creature unto itself," Sanchez said with a smile. "Anyway, if you need someone to take over piloting this rig...."

"I'll fly it, myself," Danny replied giving her a wink.

"Suit yourself," she said and then pushed her way back to towards the con.

Danny completed his report before heading to the medical bay. He figured that Doc needed some time to work and Danny being in the cramped space would not be helpful. The bay was a small room off of the chow hall. Though small, it was jammed pack with medical gear. The doctor could do pretty much any surgery they would need. At the moment, Gramps was sitting in a chair that folded out from the wall. The doctor was facing the opposite wall where a computer panel was seated. Her long, brown hair hovered above her head.

"What's the verdict?" Danny asked as he floated in front of the door. "Is he still a human?"

"Far as I can tell. Couldn't find a heart, though, and his brain was in the wrong orifice," the doctor said without turning around.

"Is he cleared for flight?"

The doctor turned to look at Danny. "I can't find a thing wrong with him. There aren't any signs of sleep-sickness. From a medical standpoint, he's good to go."

"How do you feel," Danny asked as he turned to look at Gramps.

Gramps was more floating above the chair than sitting on it. His limbs were loose and his gaze was fixed on the floor. "One part scared, two parts pissed off," he replied.

"Pissed off?" Danny said.

Gramps looked up. "At the world, in general. I don't remember doing anything that would cause a huge change in thrust attitude during a parking maneuver. I certainly don't remember turning any of our drones off."

"I believe you. I'm having engineering tearing apart the navigation and engine systems to see if there's a bug or control failure. I'm sure they'll get it fixed in no time." Danny turned back to the doctor. "Is he free to go?"

"Yup. If he needs me, you know where I work," she replied.

"Thanks, Doc," Gramps said. He unbuckled the seat and pushed off toward the door following Danny into the chow hall.

"I have something that might help distract you," Danny said.

"Oh?"

Danny gently pushed a pad over his shoulder. Gramps caught it and began to thumb through the document that was on the screen. "Our dear Chief's guess on where we'll need to place the nuke to crack this nut," Danny said.

"Anyone started the betting pool yet?"

"I haven't shown it to anyone else. I don't think betting on this one is in the best taste, considering the whole world-ending potential."

"Fair enough," Gramps said. "For the record, I would bet on him."

"He has a high success rate. What do you make of the strong magnetic field this thing is putting out?"

"Got me," Gramps said. "I'd assume there's a large vein of ferric material that runs the length of the asteroid. If it isn't near the surface then we shouldn't have a problem. If it is...."

"Then we're going to have a hard year ahead of us," Danny finished. "We'll know tomorrow. The science folks are setting up the impactor experiments."

Day 3
0830 hours

The term "impactor experiment" was really just shooting a super-dense projectile at the asteroid at a very high speed. The drones then analyze the bits of rock that spray off the asteroid to give the crew a better idea of what they will be mining. It's the closest thing the ship had to a weapon and the science guys really got a kick out of using it.

The *Lucky Strike* carried four aluminum sabots around tungsten discs designed for maximum penetration and spread. They would be fired using a railgun. The technology was as old as space exploration; but why fiddle with something that works?

Danny was strapped in to his captain's chair and Gramps was at the helm. The engineers had found nothing wrong with the navigation equipment and there was, still, no explanation as to why the ship was behaving oddly.

Danny looked over at the science station where they were preparing the impactor. "How's it coming?"

"We should be good," said the lead scientist, a short and skinny Asian man. "We have a firing solution ready."

"Lock it down," Danny said.

"Navigation is locked," Gramps said and made a show of putting his hands on his head.

"Send it," Danny ordered

With a short whine, the impactor was thrown with considerable force into space. Danny waited for the all-clear from the science personnel. He, at least, expected some hushed discussion about how well the ejector did. He only received silence.

"What are the results?" he asked.

"Umm," the man said. "We missed."

"We missed?" Danny replied. "How in the ever-loving-hell could we miss a thing that big at this range?! We've never missed a shot!" He mashed the communication button on his panel. "Engineering, what happened?"

"The issue wasn't in the railgun. Our port thrusters fired for a quarter second."

Danny looked over to Gramps who still had his hands on his head. "I'm a quick stick, boss, but I can't fire a quarter second burst with my hands on my head."

"There was, also, a modulation in the magnetic field that may have affected the course of the impactor before the sabot was shed," said one of the scientists.

"May have? And how would an asteroid change its magnetic field?" Danny demanded.

"The modulation wasn't particularly strong. We're running simulations to see if that could have pushed the impactor away," replied the lead scientist. "As to your second question, I have absolutely no idea."

"Gramps," Danny said. "Log the impactor as a potential navigation hazard. We're out in the boondocks, but rules are rules."

"Done and done," Gramps replied.

"How long before you'd want to try again?" Danny asked.

"We can do it right away," the lead scientist said. "I'd prefer to get a bit closer, though."

"Gramps, you heard the man."

"Yup," he said. "I'm going to use maneuvering thrusters only. Shouldn't be a lot of g's but we should rig for them just in case."

"Roger," Danny said and he pushed the main communications circuit. "Strap down. We're about to maneuver laterally."

The red lights on Danny's table quickly turned green as everyone strapped down. Once the board was completely green, he nodded at Gramps.

"Here we go," Gramps said as he took control back from the computer. He thrusted starboard for ten seconds, causing a light pull on the crew. The ship inched closer to the asteroid. He shut the port thrusters down and let the momentum do the work. "Approaching 40,000 meters. How close do you want?"

"30,000 meters should be sufficient," the lead scientist said.

"Roger that," Gramps said. As the ship approached the 35,000 meter mark, Gramps thrusted to port to begin cancelling out the ship's movement so that it was running alongside the asteroid at a constant rate. "We're running straight at 34,994 meters."

"We have a firing solution, skipper," said the lead scientist.

"Lock down navigation," Danny ordered. Gramps locked his console and put his hands back on his head. "Send it."

The impactor shot out of the tube and, 34,994 meters later, it struck the asteroid. Danny smiled for the first time in a couple of days.

"Minimal debris," the lead scientist reported. "Mostly a standard asteroid but it hit something denser than anything I've seen before."

"There was a huge flux in the magnetic field and it seems to be much weaker now," one of the scientists reported.

The lead scientist nodded, "I can't explain it but the instruments are showing a serious change. The field is much weaker now."

1600 Hours

The scientists hit the asteroid with the remaining two impactors. The final one dug into the rock deeper than the others. Still, the fluctuations in the magnetic field after each shot were confusing and they didn't have a lot of answers.

After reviewing the data for a couple of hours, the science team decided on a location to place the shaped nuclear charge. The location was only 5 meters away from where the Chief thought it would be.

Danny pushed out of his station and over to Sanchez. "How long will it take for you to place the nuke so we can crack this thing?"

"A couple of hours to tune it in for the best results and then another hour to place it properly. So, let's say we will be ready by 0200 hours," Sanchez replied.

"Safe distance?"

"65,000 clicks, minimum."

"Let me know when."

"You got it. I'll fly the nuke out with the drone myself that way if it gets messed up, it's my fault."

"Works for me," Danny replied.

A little over two hours later, the nuclear warhead was attached to its drone. Sanchez flew it out of the hold and set its course toward the asteroid. She gave Danny a thumbs up once the drone was completely clear.

"Take us out to 70,000 clicks, Gramps," Danny said once everyone had belted down.

"You got it, Skipper."

Gramps repeated the procedure that he used to move the ship closer. This time there was a bit more momentum needed so a gentle pull turned into strenuous pull. Gramps never liked being close to the nuke once it was clear of the cargo hold. It took the ship a couple of hours before it got close to 70,000 meters away from the asteroid. Gramps engaged thrusters for a minute or two and then brought them down to a low level so the crew could rest. To stop, he used the navigation thrusters with increasing power the closer the ship got to its goal.

Finally, Gramps turned to look at Danny. "70,000 clicks, skipper."

Danny nodded. "Lieutenant Sanchez, feel free to make it glow at your leisure."

"I've got it exactly where the science folks want it. Detonation in 10 seconds," she replied.

Danny put the image of the asteroid on his monitor. There was a small pinpoint of light that grew more and more intense until his screen automatically dimmed its output.

"Confirmed detonation with peak energy," Sanchez said.

As the light died down, the asteroid's shape came back in focus. A large crack ran down the asteroid laterally and there was much more ejecta than when they used the impactors. Danny peered at the image and engaged maximum zoom. *That cannot be real,* he thought. "Is anyone else seeing this?"

The room was as quiet as he'd ever heard it. Finally, one of the scientists said, "It's… hollow. We're picking up several canister-like objects."

"Are those decks?" Sanchez said.

A beeping sound came over the communications line indicating a message from outside the ship. Danny stared at his pad not sure what to do.

"You, uh, you should probably answer that," Sanchez suggested.

Danny pressed the communications button and had it piped in so everyone else could hear it. "This is Captain Danny Mierdah of the mining vessel *Lucky Strike.* To whom am I speaking?"

There was a pause and then, right before Danny was going to repeat his hail, a screeching voice came through, "I am computer operating lifeboat."

Danny mouthed the word, 'lifeboat' to the scientists who all shrugged helplessly. "Lifeboat?"

"I am the custodian of this lifeboat. Our home was destroyed. Only things to live are in the lifeboat. Enough to rebuild on planet in this system."

Danny blanched. "We believed you were an asteroid that would destroy that world. We had colonized it nearly a century ago. Where did you come from?"

Danny's pad showed a map of the galaxy. It quickly zoomed out, centered in one a star and zoomed back in on it.

"That's… that's seven thousand lightyears away from here!"

"Yes," the voice said. "Lifeboat would enter orbit and seed planet."

"Why didn't you warn us?! We could have helped you!" Danny said.

"Direct communication only recently possible after reading your library. Tried to deter you. Changed your course. Deactivated your drones. Used shields to block your missiles. Still, you came."

Danny sat silently and felt like he was going to vomit. After a few moments, he said, "Is there anything we can do to fix this?"

"The nuclear weapon irradiated that which it didn't destroy. I am all that is left. My power supply is low and my system is failing."

"There must be something!"

"Remember us," it said, its link becoming weak. "Remember us."

Danny watched as the asteroid changed its course just enough to have it clear the planet, trailing a debris field behind it.

"Hello?" Danny said. He waited for a couple of minutes and then repeated it, "Hello? Can you hear me?"

The radio was silent. He wasn't sure what to do next. Who should he talk to or what report should he write? He didn't know but he had a year to think about it.

YOUTH

Judi Fleming

THOMAS LOVED THE INTERNET. IT WAS THE EASIEST WAY TO SEND OUT misinformation and wage war against research. His research specifically. No reason why anyone should be concerned about what he did. Especially those bent on stopping him. He was frightened now that he knew big pharma had him in their cross hairs. At times, he worried that it was the cross hairs in the scope of a rifle. Had he remembered to lock the door to his research clinic? Yes, he was sure. He had work to do this evening and settled himself into his comfortable leather office chair in front of his old-fashioned computer.

All he had to do now was to sway public opinion and help them make him a has-been. After all, it was his experience that many people made too many decisions based upon a few fleeting facts and then clung to their suppositions and misinformation as if their life depended on it. He laughed bitterly. That's what got him into this pickle to begin with. Most people were swayed by the popular opinion of the moment and closely followed carefully selected favorite topics. Or the belief that most people were good. Yeah right. Thomas knew better now and he knew big pharma regularly used this to their advantage when dealing with the masses, telling them what to believe and what to buy.

He looked at the back of his hands as he paused in his typing. Young, strong hands. He caressed the skin, marveling in its elasticity and the absence of age spots before he forced himself to get back to work, tapping the keys as he drafted his next bit of current opinion.

He typed, "Dr. Thomas Eschere has no proof that his ridiculously named 'Baby's Breath' formula restores youth. Show me the research!"

Thomas switched user accounts and typed, "It's a sin against God and nature to tamper with DNA!"

He went down through his list of accounts, praising himself as the savior of mankind for his discovery with one, but countering it with ten other "voices" calling him a fraud and his work a crime against nature, dangerous, and more.

"What happens when people live forever? How can our world support the population growth?"

"The cure for cancer and every other disease! Praise be to God."

"No long-term data exists to see what mutations will arise out of this new product. We cannot move forward until the scientific community ensures we are not creating monsters."

"It's against God's will to manipulate humans. Stop Dr. Eschere now before we feel God's wrath!"

"There is no scientific evidence that this cellular regeneration can be sustained. The body's own cells are programmed to age. Will those following this course of treatment just fall over dead one day in their beautiful, young bodies?"

He read the news stream for a few minutes, watching the topic morph and expand. Comments spun off, speculating that there was probably some counter-treatment that would create extremely fast aging and death, which was quickly squashed as the tide of popular opinion called it evil and the human trials should stop. Some things were just too dangerous. The Trans had the answers to everything and people should be grateful for what they had. Instant information and endless entertainment. Lives were already long enough to enjoy all these things. He sat back and brushed his hands across the papers on his desk. This information was not available. All his research notes were hand written. Spread out in front of him like a fan of possibilities.

Thomas still liked the old-fashioned feel of an actual keyboard and the soft glow of his monitor. Some of his fellow researchers had switched completely to the Trans. He didn't like the computer talking back to him, to hang on his every word, and even anticipate what he'd say next. He didn't want to be swallowed whole by a virtual reality, transparent to the workings of the real world, so he stuck with what he was comfortable with. How ironic, he thought as he changed the world around him. To him, the Trans felt like a walking video game. Kids today couldn't step out of it. He rarely wore the Trans lenses, allowing his eyes to race across the sound board, ever present in his field of vision.

He liked the click of the individual keys. The movement of his hands soothed him now that the stiffness and slack skin of old age were gone. No need for all this new tech. He once again typed as fast as he had back when he was a grad student, just starting his work on cytokines and stem cells.

Oh, how the time had flown. DNA research was a marvelous thing. A field of study to which there was no end. Once the ban was lifted on genetically modified organisms and the lawyers had their day, scientists like him were free to experiment with willing test subjects. He'd been instrumental in pushing that popular opinion until it had swayed the courts. Now there were no more lengthy peer-reviewed ethics panels on human testing. No more patients dying while they waited for years long research studies to be completed and then reviewed for even more years.

All those years ago one of his online personalities had asked, "Why not allow those who wanted to take their chances to do so?" It was common sense that the masses could follow. Pharmaceutical research institutions had been overwhelmed with volunteers once the courts had made their ruling.

Then, it had been easy for him to find the people willing to try out his cytokines. Oh sure, there had been those he couldn't save, but he had saved hundreds of those participating in his first big clinical trial.

Some volunteers had even been healthy people. Those self-diagnosed hypochondriacs that the Trans proliferated as they looked up symptoms and saw themselves suffering. They'd been the key for finding what made healthy people young again. Once he'd perfected the dosage that reversed aging in the healthy, he then found the correct dosages that stopped a myriad of diseases. From schizophrenia, to major depression, Alzheimer's disease, systemic inflammatory response syndromes, to multi organ failure associated with intra-abdominal catastrophe. Even cancer. He was still stunned by that one.

Thomas typed out a few more scalding lines of text, berating the courts for not protecting the innocent. There were those who weren't smart enough to look after themselves. He chewed his lip, carefully navigating through data streams as he pushed up comments to the proliferation engines, paying the outrageous fees to spike those opinions, allowing them to bubble to the most popular Trans news-feeds.

His research had found that tiny little key which linked cytokines as the engine for the change in the stem cells, making them the trigger that removed all the aged cells in a human body. Every type of cell, from muscle to skin to internal organs, continuously refreshing them. A veritable fountain of youth.

A simple asthma inhalator had been the vehicle to administer the final product after all the research and refinement had been done. No need to draw blood and spend weeks culturing cells followed by careful, but tedious treatment routines to put the genetically modified product back into the body.

His interchangeable cartridges were tiny, self-contained laboratories. Set the switch and exhale into the device, then wait four hours as the mutations were added and proliferated. Then switch it to inhale and puff in his Cytostems®.

He found that if a person followed this course of treatment once a week for two months and you'll notice your skin has become smooth and wrinkle free, your knees no longer ached, and your spine is just a little straighter. Follow this once-a-week treatment for a year and you will be young again.

Now pharma wanted his patents. Wanted to buy him out and tuck it all away in a vault. Who would be left to treat after all, once everyone was young and healthy again? It made his head ache thinking about it. Why had he not foreseen this? He stopped. When was the last time he'd actually had a real headache? No more aspirin was available on the market.

Sweat beaded on his forehead. Why had they allowed him to live so long? He was destroying their entire business model. Oh sure, there would still be people who got hurt, birth defects to correct, but the sheer reduction of disease and illness would wipe out the pharmaceutical medical industries. Hospital systems would become obsolete. Education systems would flounder. After all, why would you need whole fields of training and education for the medical professions, not to mention all the money universities got from donors who were the doctors they created. Sheesh. He was in deep shit.

Thomas checked the masking program he had paid so much for. As rich as he was, pharma was richer. Public opinion in the Trans was gaining speed, trashing his reputation. He could erase himself there and become a has-been, but how could he hide from the companies his discovery could destroy?

The knock at his door nearly made him piss his pants. He blanked the screen and composed himself, taking deep breaths. Who the hell could it be? He hadn't scheduled any meetings this evening and he really should be on his way home by now.

The knock came again. A sharp staccato noise that made his throat tighten and he squeaked, "Who is it?"

"Dr. Eschere, we'd like to speak with you for a few minutes, if you don't mind." The voice was pleasantly professional.

Thomas stood, clenching his fists, his breath coming rapidly now. He recognized this voice. The one that left messages telling him not to put off the meeting requests any longer. Over and over. And didn't the last one say that they'd be in touch? Soon? Dammit, was it yesterday or last week that he had listened to that voice message?

The lock clicked and the door swung open. Several men and women stood in the doorway. Clean-cut people right out of a fashion magazine ad.

"May we come in? We have an offer we believe you would be hard-pressed to refuse."

"Uh, um. I, I, um don't think I could stop you, now could I?" Thomas stuttered as he eyed the clean lines of clothing, which did little to conceal the weapons tucked here and there on a few of the individuals.

The man in the center of the other six smiled a knowing, reassuring smile. Thomas noted that the smile was so perfectly executed that it even reached his eyes.

"Of course you could, but I don't think you would really want to." He gestured and the others moved forward like an assault team. Brief cases came out and Thomas's desk was cleared and rearranged with carefully prepared legal documents.

Thomas felt his knees shake and sat down abruptly. "What's all this?"

"An offer you can't refuse, Dr. Eschere. We don't want to put you out of business," he smiled reassuringly again as Thomas's head snapped up to make eye contact. "We simply want to make a mutually beneficial business arrangement. Allow us time to rework our business model, so to speak."

"I'm not selling out. I've told you that before." His throat was dry now as the two larger men on the edge of the group flexed their muscles as they crossed their arms.

Criminy, just like in the movies. Thomas thought. He took a deep breath, "I can save so many lives," he said, determined to do just that. "So many people can benefit from my discoveries. Cytostems® actually works. Look at me. For crying out loud, I'm 65, not 25."

"We know, Dr. Eschere. We know. But do you really want everyone to be young and strong again? Think of those in prison. Those who have committed horrendous crimes. Think of those countries who have named us a nation of demons and have sworn to destroy us. Think of the drug lords with their never-ending supplies of drugs and people who live forever with those addictions. Think of the consequences."

Thomas sat back, jaw agape. Why *hadn't* he thought of this? Why could he only think of his kid brother, dead now for twenty years of non-small cell lung cancer? He could have been saved if only.... He jerked himself back to here and now.

This man was right. It wasn't about him. There would be whole populations of young, strong, angry people at war. His worries about over population and lack of resources were one thing. But populations could be wiped out so easily in this era of super weapons and in-stant information. How could the average person entertain themselves through decades of extra life even with the Trans there to amuse them with endless cute cat photos and other mindless drivel? No, that wasn't what he had created this for.

The man sat down across from his desk, his smile now dazzling. "I see you understand. So let me go over this agreement with you. The first part is to stop the clinical trials."

Thomas nodded. There were only twelve hundred in the study. He could revoke the drug licensing request. None of the product had ever left this clinic. He'd been so careful about that, administering each dose himself to ensure security.

"Which drug company are you with, or do you represent them all, Mister...?" Thomas asked.

"Just call me Mr. Smith. No, I'm not with pharma if that is what you think. They're interested in your product as well, but I'm hoping you've recognized that they'd just lock up the formula."

Thomas nodded. "So who do you represent?"

"Well, think of the company I work for as a brain trust. We look for inventions that improve mankind. Ways to keep the idiots in check, so to speak." Mr. Smith turned one of the copies of contract around to face himself. "You'll see that we still allow you full rights to your discoveries. You can even manufacture personal stores of the product for a very select group of friends and family. We'll even track those in your study to see what the effects of withdrawing treatment will be."

Thomas nodded again. "So what's the catch? There's always some fine print that will get me."

"No catch really. We're going to create a work around. Build a new self-contained manufacturing plant to make a sort of retro e-cigs product like the ones people used in the twenty-first century. This makes it dissimilar enough from your original product and avoids pesky government regulations on new drugs. We'll market it as soothing for the throat as a 'dietary supplement' to avoid the government regulations on new drugs. This will make it a more affordable product for the masses."

"But I thought you just said you didn't want the average person to have this," Thomas quirked his eyebrows trying to figure what this group was angling for.

"Oh, we will control the product, releasing it to those brilliant minds deemed worthy. We just want it to be normal to see it being used. Making mass market product will recoup some of the money we'll be paying you."

He pointed to a line on the contract and Thomas looked down at the figure and bolted to his feet, chocking and coughing. "You're going to pay me that much?!" He ran both hands through his hair and gripped it at the top of his skull. "This makes no sense. You could just walk back into the lab and take it all right now. I can't stop you." Thomas dropped his hands to his side. "Come on, Mr. Smith, what's the catch? What do you need me alive for?"

Mr. Smith smiled through steepled fingers. "Why, Dr. Eschere, we simply need a variation on your product. Your research into cytokines suggest that you could also make a formulation which speeds the aging process of internal organs, enhancing that intra-abdominal catastrophe effect that cytokines sometimes do all on their own right now. We'll need to make the retro e-cigs popular enough so when a select few receive a special order of those particular beauties on one will notice. World peace and all, you see."

Mr. Smith's eyes were cold and clear and the smile on his face was now deadly serious.

MEETING THE OTHER

Nancy Jane Moore

"I'M CONCERNED THAT WE HAVEN'T SEEN ANY INDICATION OF SETTLE-ments anywhere on the planet," the exobiologist said.

Starfire picked up the images that went with those words and began to listen. Up to that point, it hadn't been paying close attention to the meeting. Even though humans had perfected mind-to-mind communication since meeting Cibolans three quarters of a century back, they still insisted on speaking out loud most of the time. As far as Starfire was concerned, that practice caused miscommunication. It wasn't just that most speakers edited what they said — that was true of telepathic communication, too — it was that spoken words lacked enough context to be precise. But as the only Cibolan on the expedition to the H-17 System, Starfire had developed its own workarounds. In meetings, it left one part of its mind free to pay attention to the mental background noise that accompanied each person's conversation and behind a block, thought about other things.

"If there's intelligent life down there," the exobiologist went on, "it doesn't resemble anything else we've seen."

Two civilizations don't provide enough data to form a theory on what intelligent life might look like, Starfire thought. Cibolans were the only other form of intelligent life humans had seen, and the two species were more alike than different, an understanding that had become clear to Starfire when it spent five years studying xenology on Earth. But it agreed with the substance of what the exobiologist was saying both out loud and mentally: *Wait.*

Everyone on board knew the captain was ready to send down an exploratory team. Starfire hadn't expected anyone but itself to raise concerns. During the two-year trip to the H-17 System from its home planet of Cibola in the Doradoan system, it had become accustomed to the human habit of kowtowing to the authority of the Solar System military on any expedition they operated. The captain would make the final decision, regardless. Because of that, many of those who had concerns kept quiet.

Starfire did a quick mental scan of the room and read general agreement with the exobiologist. But no one else appeared to be ready to speak. It took a few moments to craft a sentence—speaking was much more difficult for Cibolans than mind communication was for humans—and then said, "We should observe more before we go. They may not welcome us." It accompanied its words with a rush of images, conveying the risk of jumping in without all the information available. The human ship had amazing machines for scanning the planet from a distance; more should be done.

"From what we're getting from the scan so far there's nothing down there we can't handle," said the marine colonel. He hadn't bothered to block his thoughts and Starfire picked up the man's contempt for all things non-human.

Annoyed, Starfire responded by sending an image from the human-Cibolan war that had ended badly for their planet but worse for the humans. "You might have made a mistake," it said. "Not all civilizations are friendly."

"Hell, there's probably not anything down there at all," the colonel said.

"There is definitely something on that planet," Starfire said. "I have felt something probe my mind. Have you not felt the same?"

The colonel laughed, but a quick scan of the room showed that most of the others had noticed something.

The captain cut off discussion. "We'll send a skeleton crew to the planet," the captain said. "The key scientists—xenology, exobiology, exogeology. A pilot and shuttle crew along with a few marines. Take the ship down to a lower orbit, and get a crew down there." He stood up and the rest of the team followed suit.

Starfire walked back to its quarters with Astrid Lindholm, the shuttle pilot. She was almost as tall as the Cibolan—quite tall for a human—and similar in color, with pale white skin and white-blonde hair that complemented Starfire's bluish-silver fur. Of course, she only had two arms instead of four. *Thanks for speaking out*, she sent. *You're right about taking time, right about the mental probing, but they're not going to listen. They're too eager.* As with most humans, her sending was a mix of images and words, but Starfire could follow it.

Your people are so good at studying from a distance, it sent back. *Why not use that now?*

She nodded and shrugged, sending an image of a male gorilla beating its chest. *One of our male traditions,* she sent. *Showing we're tough.*

But not all of you are men, Starfire sent back. During its sojourn on Earth it had learned to pick up cues about people's gender, since some humans took offense if you got it wrong. However, other humans—some of whom had altered their bodies—were fascinated by the fact that Cibolan genders weren't fixed, and only came into play when partners decided to have a child.

That tough male tradition is still strong in military folks, she replied. *Even me. You are right that we should do more scans, but I'm still itching to get down there.*

One of the many unmanned ships humans had sent to check out other planetary systems for resources, potential human settlement, and intelligent life had reported back on the H-17 system. The report concluded the system contained mineral resources far beyond that of either the human Solar System or Cibolan's Doradoan System (as the humans called it). It also noted that at least one planet—labeled H-17-L—had an atmosphere similar enough to Earth's that it might be suitable for human life.

The Solar System Union had put together an expedition to the system, which was located about forty light years beyond Cibola. After the expedition was underway, the probe ship had sent one last message: It had found indications of intelligent life on the planet. The report had not been detailed and the probe had not been heard from again.

Because the original expedition had not included any xenologists, Starfire had been invited along when the ship stopped at Cibola. The humans had also extended an invitation to Starfire's spouse, Comet, an astrophysicist. But Starfire had recently given birth to their second child and Comet was now nurturing it in its pouch. Neither of them were willing to bring a baby along. Starfire had been leery of many things about the expedition, but the possibility of meeting another intelligent race overcame its objections. That desire to meet others had led it to xenology, and this might be the only opportunity in its lifetime. Comet had supported the decision, though their parting had left them both in pain.

When Starfire and Comet had discussed it, Comet had sent the image of alliance it had picked up from the scientific crew on the mission. *At least they're planning to work with the people they find.* On Cibola, the humans had started out with the idea that they would just run everything. They had learned from that mistake, at least, but they still had not learned caution.

In preparation for the shuttle trip, Starfire wrote a message to Comet to be sent by the ship's com system. It did little but convey love. The thoughts Starfire wanted to share with its spouse could not be put in human language, but they were too far apart for real communication.

According to the scans, the planet's atmosphere wasn't breathable for humans or Cibolans. The mixture of gases was similar — and conducive to carbon-based life — but there was less oxygen and more nitrogen, so all members of the landing team would wear suits and breathing masks. During its time on Earth, Starfire had used a suit to visit some of the outer planets and found it uncomfortable even though it had been specifically tailored for a Cibolan's four arms and non-human build. Even when well-designed, suits restricted movement, and Starfire was used to moving freely.

The humans seemed to feel the same way, for all of them had put their suits in the storage compartment. "We'll suit up when we get close to the planet," Astrid said.

The crew didn't chatter much on the way down. It seemed odd to Starfire, who had become accustomed to the constant sound of human communication. Nor was there much telepathic sharing. *Afraid to show weakness,* Starfire thought. These were colleagues, not family and friends; humans drew strong distinctions between those roles. As an outsider — even after two years, it remained an outsider — Starfire also blocked its worries.

Astrid and her crew spoke quietly to each other. One crew member spoke via comm to the ship in orbit, keeping them apprised of their progress. Routine communication, in case something not-routine happened. Starfire tried to go over all the information indicating there was life on the planet. It was so meagre. Had humans come to Cibola with as little knowledge? No wonder there had been so many misunderstandings between them and Starfire's people.

The shuttle was equipped with a version of the Alcubierre/Nguyen Drive, which allowed travel above light speed by expanding and contracting space. But the distance to the planet from orbit was under two hundred thousand kilometers. Sublight travel would only take a couple of days; no need to use up precious resources to get there more quickly.

They had covered about half the distance when Starfire felt a presence in its mind. It was much more powerful than the probe it had felt before—a sense that something was combing through every inch of its mind and body. Starfire could tell that the others felt it as well. When it had felt the initial probe, Starfire had been unsure whether it came from another mind or from machines like the humans used, but now it could sense a powerful intelligence of some kind. It opened its mind to the presence, and tried to read the source.

The response stunned Starfire so much that it nearly passed out. There was a mind there, no question, but such a vast one that it could not be grasped by one mind alone. Starfire tried to pull together all the minds on the shuttle to help examine it, but that proved difficult. Humans still did not train in how to work together mentally, as all Cibolans did, and the small mental weave it put together was patchy. But even if they had been working at full Cibolan-like strength, the twenty people on the shuttle, or even the hundreds on the main ship, would not have been enough to comprehend this mind. Starfire wasn't sure the entire planet of Cibola could have created a weave that could respond to this.

Starfire tried once again, pulling on the mindstrength available, to see if it could comprehend a little more, and suddenly hit a wall. The effect was physical. Starfire reeled, and at least two people fell from their seats. It wasn't just a block; it was no admittance sign, a warning, a threat. To Starfire, raised in a culture in which fights were mind-to-mind, the meaning was obvious.

Get us out of here, it sent. And then, because humans liked spoken word so much, it yelled, "Turn around, now."

But Astrid was staring at the image of the planet on the large screen at the front of the bridge. Was she injured, stunned by the threat? Worried, Starfire entered her mind. All her blocks were down and it could see her sending pleas to the entity out there: *Let us in. We mean no harm.*

Astrid. We must leave now, Starfire sent, but she didn't appear to notice him at all. Carefully—since it did not understand how to fly a complicated ship like the shuttle—it took control of her mind, made her think about turning the ship around. After half a minute, she gave an order to her crew, "Reverse course," and pressed some buttons. The ship began to come about. Starfire stayed in her head, and once they had changed direction, nudged her to bring the speed up to maximum sublight. They headed back toward the ship in orbit.

"*Madre de dios*," the comm officer said. "The main ship is powering up weapons."

"Do those idiots think they can fight that thing? We don't even know what it is," the exobiologist said.

Astrid seemed to be regaining her senses. Starfire eased back, but sent her a message: *Tell the captain to pull out of orbit and get far away. We are all in danger.*

Astrid turned to the comm officer. "Tell them to pull out of orbit and get out of range as fast as they can. We'll rendezvous once we're away from this planet."

The comm officer followed her instructions. A few minutes passed, minutes in which no one made a sound as they waited for a reply.

"They say, 'Continue escape. We will hold our ground.'"

"Bakas," said the marine sergeant. "They're in the middle of space. No ground to hold."

Images of agreement bounced around the shuttle.

"I've lost contact," the comm officer said.

"What do you mean? Comm malfunction?" Astrid asked.

"I mean there's nothing there. We're on a short delay, but I've been able to hear something all along. And now nothing."

Another crew member changed the ship's long-range camera, so that it was focused on where the mother ship was supposed to be, and put that image on screen. There was nothing there. He cursed, checked his equipment, and tried again, with the same result.

Someone else activated a long-range scanner.

Starfire reached into everyone's mind, asking them to help it reach out. They weren't that far away; they should be able to reach the ship with a strong weave.

"I think the ship is gone," the person who had run the scan was saying just as Starfire had concluded the same thing.

"I didn't hear an explosion or anything," the comm officer said. "They were just suddenly not there."

"Let's get far, far away," said the marine sergeant. "Now."

Starfire read that all twenty minds agreed.

Astrid gave the order to go to A/ND.

They came out of jump at the edge of the same system and established an orbit around the small, outer-most planet, some five billion kilometers from H-17-L. Several people activated the nanopod in the shuttle's tiny galley and produced hot drinks for all. The comm officer stayed at her post in the hope that some signal might come from their mother ship and another officer kept watch on the bridge, just in case something else might happen, but the rest of the crew found places to sit in the passenger compartment. Starfire could read a mixture of emotions in the room: fear, determination, a huge sense of loss. The marine sergeant spoke the words on everyone's minds. "What do we do now?" Everyone looked at Astrid.

Starfire picked up "why me" thoughts from her, then watched as she realized she had to take command. The scientists in the crew might be older and wiser, but they knew nothing about piloting any kind of ship. She was military and this was a military expedition. Starfire watched Astrid tamp down her own fears before she spoke. "To begin with, we need to get in touch with the Solar System Union. Our best bet is to send a message to Cibola via the A/ND comm. That will be faster than sending to Earth."

"A/ND comm takes several weeks. Wouldn't it be better to use the quantum entanglement comm? We can only send text that way, but that would work in this case." The speaker was one of the engineers.

"It would, if we had it on the shuttle. But the only ETQ device was on the mother ship. A/ND is all we've got."

"Are we safe from that — *thing* — out here? Or should we get farther away?" The speaker was the exogeologist.

Starfire got a mental message from Astrid: *Say something*. "I can no longer feel the entity," it said.

"Could it come after us?"

"I do not know," Starfire said. "I do not know what it is and what technology it may have."

"But what do you think?" the exobiologist said. He must have been picking up hints from the Cibolan's mind.

"It is possible that the entity is the entire planet," Starfire said. "It felt more like one powerful mind than a weave of many minds. But even if it does not travel outside its orbit, that does not mean that it cannot send something after us. It did something to our mother ship."

"Anyone got any idea what that was?" the marine sergeant said.

The room was quiet. Starfire read the thoughts. People were trying to come up with an optimistic theory, but it could tell that everyone thought the ship had been destroyed, with all its occupants.

Astrid said, "We are as safe here as we can be in these circumstances. We need to be near a planet or asteroid with useful elements, because we're going to need to stoke up our nanopod to make sure we've got enough food. As I recall the system scans, that planet down there fills the bill."

The exogeologist nodded.

One of the marines asked the question on everyone's mind. "Can we get home?"

Astrid shook her head. "Not in this shuttle. Our A/ND isn't big enough and, even if it was, we don't have enough fuel to travel that kind of distance. We can't even jump out of this system to another one with planets we can mine."

"So we have to just sit here and hope the SSU sends a ship for us?"

"I'm afraid so," Astrid said.

"Will they?" The marine sergeant again. "Or will they decide it's better to let us die out here than attract that entity's attention?"

The fear in the room was so strong that Starfire had to put up a block to stay focused.

Astrid shrugged.

The engineer said, "We could possibly use the nanopod to build a bigger A/ND and storage tank. If the moons around this planet have Helium-3" —he looked at the geologist, who nodded— "we could maybe build a ship that would get us home."

Starfire felt the hope. Someone else said, "That will take years, even if we can figure out how to do it."

"We've got years," another person said. "Even if they come for us, the closest A/ND ship is a good three or four years from here."

"It's good to know we have another possibility if they don't come for us, but let's see what the SSU says before we go that far," Astrid said. "Right now, we should concentrate on how to build up food stores and also create some screens and beds so we can have a bit of privacy and comfort on this ship." She gave people assignments—one for every person, Starfire noticed—and the meeting broke up.

As the others moved around the ship to begin working on their tasks, Astrid came over and sat down by Starfire. *It was you who turned the ship around,* she sent.

You did the work. I just helped you decide to do it, Starfire sent back. *I'm sorry if you felt invaded.*

No, no. I'm grateful. You saved us all. They're thanking me, but it was you who did it. I should tell them.

No. It will just make them afraid of me.

How did you know that being was dangerous? It was so vast, so exciting. I just wanted it to speak to me.

It reminded me too much of wars on Cibola, when people come together in a mental weave for harm. When it threw up that block, I was certain it would harm us if we didn't leave.

And you were right, Astrid sent.

Starfire shrugged—a human habit it had developed. *Probably.*

But didn't you want to know more about it?

Yes. Oh, yes. But it was never going to let me do that. I may never meet another alien species and all I got of this one was a glimpse. We may never be able to communicate with that being, not even if we keep evolving for millions more years. It's so different from us. And the universe could be full of others like it. The fact that humans and Cibolans are able to connect and communicate has blinded us to the reality that there are many possible life forms that we will never be able to understand. As a xenologist, it breaks my heart. But the glimpse was nice.

Worth the dangers? Worth the risk that we'll never get home?

I think so, Starfire sent. It thought about how it missed Comet and their children, but it sent again, *I think so.*

THE THIRD HEAVEN

Robert Greenberger

THEY WARNED HER. REPEATEDLY. FROM THE MOMENT ANA CLARA Andarilho applied for the deep space program, the tedium of space flight was a topic of discussion brought up with mind-numbing frequency. Every time it came up, she would smile, nod, and say, "I am a very patient person."

She never really expected to have that patience tested so severely. She had been out in space, a marvel in itself, for six months. The newness of it all faded after the first two weeks, after the thrill of leaving Earth's atmosphere, and then passing the moon, and nearing Mars. Along with eleven other passengers, she had trained for two years for this mission, which also meant there were two years to get to know each other so there was little new to learn over these last six months.

They had one another and the stars for company.

The vastness of space had been mesmerizing early on, trying to fix her gaze on a bright light and then imagine she could actually see it shift position through the windows. It was largely in her imagination so, despite their fantastic speed, the distance traveled wasn't nearly enough to actually alter the starry landscape. That was one of the tricks in the movies, that you could actually watch the stars pass by, twinkling light poles or billboards in space, creating the illusion of motion. Somewhere out there was the rock she was to stand upon.

There was another six months to go before they reached their destination, the famed Asteroid Belt, where she would be among the first humans to step foot on one of the giant, floating rocks that might have once been a planet. She'd take samples, storing most of them for later study back on Earth, and perform experiments in the lab. She held out hope it would feel like she had used her time wisely once they arrived. Daily, she would remind herself of the enormity of this accomplishment and how tiny she was against the vastness of the universe. One misstep and she would float among the stars.

For now, though, the sameness of each day had worn her down. Each cycle she would wake up, clean up, pray, and have breakfast with whoever else was awake during that shift. There were experiments in progress that needed to be checked and of course the requisite hours of exercise to maintain muscle mass. But the exercise equipment was tedium made manifest as the whirring of the stationary bikes lulled her into stupor despite whatever music or podcast she blared through her earbuds. The air circulating through their habitat section was rhythmic, a constant background noise, and any shift in tone was cause for concern.

The crew had decided before the launch, that to keep things fresh, the three four-man shifts would be frequently shuffled to better mix up who was working with whom. It prevented cliques from forming or, more dangerously, romances. No one really expected a dozen prime specimens of humanity to be celibate for such a long stretch, so the roster rotations were also to assure variety in potential partners. During these long, wearisome shifts most every member of the crew was brutally honest, confessing sins dating back to elementary school, stuff that now brought laughs rather than guilt. It helped pass the time and brought levels of trust that would be needed should things go sideways.

Staring out the window at the near-motionless stars, Ana periodically wished for some malfunction, nothing fatal, just something to break the stifling routine she was certain was robbing everyone of their psychic energy at a rate faster than their muscles might atrophy. Ana let her mind wander, losing track of time during her off-duty hours. There were so few of them that it seemed positively sinful to waste them just staring but the stars took hold of her. The blackness between the pinpricks of white light held so many mysteries. What was out there? Now that hundreds of planets had been found orbiting dozens of suns across the universe, it appeared increasingly certain that man was not alone in the universe. The thought didn't trouble the devout Catholic; the Bible provided for that eventual discovery. It was all a part of God's plan when he created the Heavens and the Earth.

She just didn't expect so *much* of it. Day after day, week after week, the stars remained vast. In fact, the universe felt magnified and endless at the same time and lately, she was feeling overwhelmed by it all. If God gave man intellect and he used that to cross the distance between worlds, it had to have been part of His plan. But, she wondered, not for the first time, what was her place in that plan? Was it to chip away at dead rock and bring samples of his extraterrestrial glory to Earth? Was it something else?

She and Carol Sanderson, an oval-faced, black-haired beauty, were sharing a meal while the other two on duty were working out. Rarely did the four eat together since the dining space was on the cramped side, something everyone cursed the engineers and designers for. Today's dinner was some Teriyaki Chicken Hash concoction that smelled better than it tasted. After years of complaints from the International Space Station, the commissary crew for this mission made certain to have pungent meals along with a substantial amount of fiery condiments. As it was, she still added Wasabi powder to the Hash to bolster its appeal.

"Do you ever wonder about destiny?" she asked Carol. The two got along well enough, although the more conservative Brazilian didn't necessarily like hearing about the commander's sexual exploits. Still, Carol was an excellent pilot and crew commander. Ana definitely respected her military background and liked having her in charge of the mission.

"Dad put me on this path," Carol said between mouthfuls. The clumpy nature of the food made it easier to manipulate, but everyone was exceptionally careful since no one wanted floating food particles in their hair or worse. "The first time he took me up flying I knew this is where I wanted to be."

"Never any doubts?"

"About my mission? My destiny?" Carol paused, choosing her words carefully. "I know you're more devout than I am, but I make my destiny, Ana. And you made yours. Never doubt that."

"But I do. Every day I look out at the stars and once the awe fades, I see how insignificant I am, we all are. And it makes me wonder."

"Don't go down that rabbit hole," Carol warned, gesturing with her fork for emphasis. "That way lies madness, Ana. I won't have a crewman lose her mind out here. You worked too hard to get here to lose track of your purpose. You're here to help us understand God's creations and making sense of the universe is a perfectly fine destiny. We all have our part to play and we are all a part of that grand design. Never lose sight of that."

Ana nodded and wanted to take comfort from her words, but when Carol left to hit the rack, she looked out the window and tried to imagine which direction was Heaven and which would lead to Hell. Without ground and sky, up and down, she felt lost. Crossing herself, she murmured a prayer and then rose, floating off to the exercise equipment. Already working up a sweat was Hassan Mahmood, their engineer or, as he put it, their janitor; the first to repair damaged equipment and always testing the gear, including the devices she would be using in a few more months. He was dark-skinned, black-haired and his eyes and teeth shone, surrounded by beading sweat.

They nodded as she strapped onto the cycle and began pumping, setting a leisurely pace as something to do after eating and so as not to cause cramps. According to the ship's rules, since he didn't have earbuds in, a conversation was not off-limits.

"Do anything new today?" The challenge by this point was finding something new to do and the crew had taken to pushing in new directions, adopting new hobbies just for the variety. In her case, she took up Sudoku a week earlier much as she hated such puzzles.

"Well, I wanted to stroll outside, but the lack of air in the weather report scuttled those plans," he said archly.

"You'd enjoy that, wouldn't you? Walking in the vacuum?"

"I would, yeah. Not just for the variety, but to actually be in space, not in a tin can hurtling through space."

"Well, to do it right, you'd need to ditch the suit."

"True, but then it would be a very brief, very painful experience. I'll compromise with the suit."

"And if something went wrong, and you died…?"

"I'd feel like an idiot."

"A dead idiot. Would you worry about being separated from the ship?"

"You mean disconnected, unable to regain a handhold? I'd tumble away as the ship continued."

"And you'd be lost. A lost, dead idiot." She paused then asked, "And if you died, does your soul know where to go?"

He perceptibly slowed down, studying her carefully, looking to see if she was still teasing him. Her eyes met his and showed her serious intent.

"I'm not much on religion, Ana, you know that. But, yeah, if there's a Heaven, my soul would know where to go."

"How?"

He stared at her and must have recognized the need in her expression so he gave it some more thought, wiped a forearm across his forehead, and answered her. "Heaven and Hell is not up and down. That's a convenience because the sky on Earth is at best a promise of the stars and presumably Heaven beyond them. But those realms can't be in this universe so they're someplace else and as a result, once we transcend this existence, we find our new home."

"How can you be certain?"

"Isn't that what your faith is all about? Believing those worlds await the souls?"

She supposed that made sense but if space were that vast and endless, she was afraid she'd still be lost, denied that transcendence. Whenever she thought about stepping onto the asteroid, a part of her imagined the rock moving and she'd tumble off it, tumbling, lost in all that emptiness. Physically, she'd be a piece of space debris but it was her immortal soul's direction that worried her the most.

Over the next few days, she continued to talk with members of the crew, asking them what they thought about the existence and location of Heaven and Hell. She made certain to be casual about it, but clearly, aboard such a small space, it was obvious she was having issues. It wasn't that she was a religious fanatic, but took it seriously. She prayed each day, followed the calendar for the High Holy Days. She observed Lent, such as it was. When Christmas came, the crew exchanged little things they had packed in advance, on advice from NASA, which was much derided until those tiny touches of home were revealed and then more than a few tears were shed.

Still, Carol sought out Ana one evening, even though the commander should have been asleep. It had been a stressful day, one that proved you had to be careful for what you wished for. Several circuits blew at once, ruining one experiment and panicking the crew. Hassan and James Woo spent hours tracing the cause, replacing fuses, and then testing the major systems. Everyone's routine was disrupted, which was a relief on one hand, and a concern on the other because things could have been much worse.

Ana was cleaning up in the galley when Carol floated in and grabbed a handrail to slow her momentum and then smoothly slid into the chair. Everyone had gotten good at the acrobatics involved and there were even some competitions – men versus women, military versus civilian, American versus the World – and it certainly helped the mood and gave people something to strive for.

"How are you doing, Ana?"

"Fine, I guess. Am I not doing fine?" She finished wiping a counter, tucked away the microfiber cloth, and joined her at the table.

"As a member of the crew, you're fine. You've done nothing wrong, but as a member of the human race, you're kind of freaking out."

She frowned at that but understood the concern. Clearly, asking everyone about Heaven meant they were talking among themselves. The worry was a natural concern especially if there was any belief she might do something to herself, the crew, or even the ship.

"You think I'm going crazy?"

Carol's hands enveloped Ana's and she looked down, noting the differing skin tones, even after months without direct sunlight. Skin care was something everyone, men and women, worried about in the relatively dry air of the spaceship. The hands were dry as a result, but also warm and comforting. There wasn't much public physical contact so this was a pleasant surprise for her.

"Not crazy, no. But your preoccupation with dying and where your soul goes can lead you to a dark place. We all go through periods where we question our existence, but out here, we don't have time to let things get out of hand. If you're really struggling with your place in the universe, it's fine to ask and talk about it."

"Just so as I don't obsess and appear like a religious fanatic," Ana said in a low voice.

"You're not a zealot. I know the difference between devout and zealotry as do you. But you clearly need someone to talk to, who understands the scriptures as well as you do and I don't think the rest of us are up to it."

"We're not exactly close to a confessional," Ana cracked.

"No, but you can chat with Xander."

Ana looked up, meeting Carol's steady eyes. The ship's A.I., nicknamed Xander by one of its programmers, was not something she would have considered. To her, it was a pleasant interface but she knew it was merely data processing to replicate humanity. It didn't feel or have faith.

"What good will that do?"

"Xander controls our library which includes countless works on every subject. Hell, I randomly asked it about botany yesterday and learned facts about flora that I never heard before. Really, Ana, talk to Xander and see what the repository of human knowledge has to say. Maybe it'll help, maybe not."

"And this way, I stop bugging everyone else," Ana interjected.

"No, maybe it will give you new things to consider and then talk to us some more," Carol said. "Ana, I need you comfortable with your place here on this ship. We've got a long way to go before we reach our objective and then a longer return. I don't just need you physically fit, but mentally fit, too. If you keep on this track…well, I am concerned."

Ana nodded, feeling wounded by the words while still enjoying the human contact. She was sure the crew was freaked out by her much as the universe had pushed her closer to the edge. And Carol was right, they were better off if she could find some way to get comfortable with being in space.

"Fine, I'll talk to Xander and see how it goes. I really want to be good with all of this," Ana replied.

"I know you do."

There was one small space that was designed for privacy beyond the crew's personal bunk space. It was intended for private communications from Earth or contemplation or prayer and Ana had taken advantage of it now and then, usually on Sundays when she would quietly read the Bible and conduct her version of Mass. A chat with her priest made it clear she could not receive communion in space and she didn't think the wine would survive the trip anyway. She did the prayers and followed the reading schedule he did provide her, complete with links to recommended homilies related to the readings. It wasn't the same as being with everyone and none of the other crew were devout enough to join her weekly. A few did gather for Christmas and Easter but now that they were in Ordinary Time, it was just her.

Now, she sat in the gray-white space, the chair comfortable beneath her and she fingered her rosary beads as she clutched her Bible (paper not digital) in the other hand. Stealing herself for what promised to be a very odd conversation, she said, "Hello, Xander." At the code words, the display lit up and an image of Earth appeared, one the crew took soon after leaving orbit.

"Hello, Ana."

"The commander suggested I talk to you about my religious concerns."

"I am not a priest," the male voice said. There had been a debate about asking a celebrity to provide the voice but when the crew couldn't agree, they went with an anonymous voiceover actor. "I am also not a rabbi or an imam."

"I know, but she thought you might help me find my way."

"Are you lost?"

"Not physically, spiritually," she said calmly.

"I see. Are we speaking about temporal or metaphysical issues?"

"Do you believe there is a Heaven?"

"The majority of organized faiths on Earth recognize a realm where spirits or souls go after life on the planet ends," Xander replied.

"Do you have a personal opinion?" She felt foolish asking, but needed to hear something other than a canned response.

"I have never been asked that before, Ana. I am not certain other than the preponderance of literature suggests mankind wants to believe in something after death."

"What happens to you after the mission ends?"

"Should we safely return to Earth, my program will likely be preserved as is and then cloned for upgrades for the next mission so you could say that I will be reborn in a new form."

She hadn't considered reincarnation for software, but it made sense.

"What troubles you?"

"It's one thing to read about how large the universe is and it's something else entirely to be out among the stars and feel totally insignificant. I feel lost out here, uncertain about my place."

"When reality exceeds expectations, it is common to feel overwhelmed. You have been out here for six months and five days. It is natural that the routine leads to these feelings. It appears a perfectly normal reaction."

"Then why do I feel so lost?"

"I cannot answer that," Xander said. She had hoped to hear compassion but the response was flat. She sat in silence for several seconds and began to rise when it spoke again.

"You have your Bible with you. That is His word and it begins with Genesis. The book is a story of His creation which is, after all, the entire universe."

She sat back down.

"The Bible was the first book to say the world was round, long before man could prove it was so. Man has been revising his beliefs about the world and how it works since he first gained sentience. The Bible, though, has not been substantively revised. Retranslated, yes, rewritten for common tongues, but the basic tenets have not altered."

"Yes," she said, suddenly very interested in what Xander had to offer.

"There are countless cultures with creation myths from the Altaics who thought the world resided on the backs of three giant fish, similar to the Hindu belief the world was supported by four elephants. The Bible, though, established that Earth resided on nothing."

"Nothing?"

"In Job 26:7, it states that God 'hangs the earth on nothing.' The vacuum of space has often been considered 'nothing'."

"That nothing is the universe," she said.

"That is what the Bible says. It goes on to say in Isaiah 40:22 'It is he who sits above the circle of the earth, and its inhabitants are like grasshoppers; who stretches out the heavens like a curtain, and spreads them like a tent to dwell in.'"

"The expanding universe," she said quietly, feeling a sense of awe, especially considering she has constantly read the Bible but never paused to collect all it had to say about space. Xander, though, could more instantaneously seek out the revelations. She was fascinated.

Ana had to report for her work shift, so she thanked Xander and asked it to save its findings for their next conversation. She floated out of the small chamber, feeling better than she had in some time.

Over the next week, she scheduled time in the privacy space to continue her conversations with Xander. Between visits, she did her work, slept peacefully for a change, and continued to stare out into space, but no longer felt quite so overwhelmed. These stars and gaseous clouds and debris were all part of His work and she was there to glory in it, not be lost.

She still remained uncertain about finding Heaven in the advent of her death and that continued to weigh on her. At least, she thought, she was no longer freaking out her crewmates. No one brought it up, but the looks in their eyes showed a certain sense of relief.

"Xander, is there life on other worlds?" Ana asked one afternoon.

"None has been found," it replied. "With every new world discovered in the Goldilocks zone, however, there is an increased likelihood such life exists."

"What does the Bible say on the subject?"

"Nothing specific, although Isaiah 40:26 suggests other life may exist."

"Can you quote it for me?"

"Lift up your eyes on high and see: who created these? He who brings out their host by number, calling them all by name, by the greatness of his might, and because he is strong in power not one is missing."

"That's kind of vague," she said after considering the quote.

"Psalm 19:1-6 might support the supposition," Xander said then began reciting. "To the choirmaster. A Psalm of David. The heavens declare the glory of God, and the sky above proclaims his handiwork. Day to day pours out speech, and night to night reveals knowledge. There is no speech, nor are there words, whose voice is not heard. Their voice goes out through all the earth, and their words to the end of the world. In them he has set a tent for the sun, which comes out like a bridegroom leaving his chamber, and, like a strong man, runs its course with joy."

"Would not the Heavens suggest the Heavenly Host, the angels?"

"That is but one interpretation, Ana. It could mean life among the stars."

"So, there is nothing specific about God creating an alien Adam and Eves elsewhere?"

"Nothing so specific," Xander admitted. The tonelessness of the voice could be irritating and she hoped its next iteration improved on that. Still, it once more gave her things to consider.

"Wait a second," she said, recalling something. She thumbed through her Bible and found the passage that she had read only weeks earlier. "Psalm 115 says, 'The heavens are the Lord's heavens, but the earth he has given to the children of Man.' Doesn't that sound like we're the only lifeforms in the universe?"

"The children of Man, yes. But life, as you know, takes many different shapes. It could be the sentient life elsewhere in the universe was not made in God's image but instead similar to the creatures he created prior to Man."

She was left to ponder that, certain she would come back for more conversations. After all, when it came to her beliefs, only Xander seemed to fully comprehend the larger issues troubling her. Julianna, Carol, and Maksim were sympathetic but admitted they were all lapsed while Max, who was a Jew, vaguely knew that rabbis through the centuries did not discount the notion of life on other worlds. The Torah did not definitively discount the notion while it did not explicitly say so. And while Judaism didn't subscribe to the Christian notion of Heaven and Hell, he reassured her that they did believe in a world to come. He promised he'd do some research and while she could ask Xander, she wanted to see how serious he would be about it.

She and Xander had been talking for three weeks and she was absorbed by their conversations, which had gone beyond merely quoting scripture at one another, as they explored the core beliefs. In fact, Ana was getting teased about having an affair with the machine and that actually led to Maksim hitting on her for the first time when they recently shared the night shift. It was tempting but she needed to make sure her head was straight before letting her body go exploring.

No sooner had she sat down for their latest session when Xander surprised her with, "What are your core beliefs?"

She hesitated, ordering them in her mind. "I guess I believe in the Ten Commandments and doing God's work on Earth. I believe in hard work. I like to play hard, too, I guess. Why are you asking?"

"Between our sessions I have been replaying the conversations and am trying to compile new information to accompany your psychological profile so I can better assist you."

Ana wasn't certain she knew the ship's A.I. could actually adapt on the fly, and she was at first pleased it was working so hard, but also a little alarmed, having also read way too much dystopian fiction about artificial intelligence run amok.

"Do you know how these beliefs were forged?"

"My parents were taking me to Church while I was still in the womb," she cracked. "We were all very devout in my family. Everyone went to Church and we lived a very faithful life. Our family parties were infused with prayers as a part of the celebration. We burned more candles than we ate candy, I think."

"Did it help you grow up?"

"It gave me faith and strength, I suppose. It was tough in Brazil. Even in the 21st century, the county was very male-dominated. Women were secondary to the whims of the men. When money got tight, there was enough for my brother to go to university, but they legitimately questioned if I needed it.

"You know, Xander, I had to fight for everything. We scrambled for the last portion of *moqueca* at home and I had to argue with the counselors to take the harder math and science courses. When there were only so many slots, women were under-represented and it was an argument *every year*. It was almost the same at university so when I got to travel abroad and got to study at Johns Hopkins' Applied Physics Lab it was heavenly. I wasn't the only girl or nearly the only one. It opened my eyes. Still, when I graduated and stayed in America to work, I saw how male-dominated the sciences remained. I was disappointed but it made me work harder, to be better so when I saw something, I could obtain it."

"Was it the same with the space program?"

"Sort of. Being an international cooperative, women were far better represented, but just to get considered was a struggle since men outnumbered women applicants."

"Your accomplishments must fill you with pride."

Now Xander was sounding like a psychiatrist and if it asked about her mother or father she was done.

"Yeah, it did. But it was my faith that got me through the toughest parts."

"But now your faith isn't enough?"

"I guess not."

"What has changed? This is a new struggle, to be sure, but it remains little different than all the obstacles between your home and your place aboard the ship."

"I don't know."

"It appears, Ana, that your faith was there at the beginning and is there for when your life ends, but we're now in the middle, on a path without a real map. Could this be why you feel so lost?"

"Maybe."

"'Remember those earlier days after you had received the light, when you endured in a great conflict full of suffering."

"What's that from?"

"Hebrews 10:32," Xander said. "'You need to persevere so that when you have done the will of God, you will receive what he has promised, for "in just a little while, he who is coming will come and will not delay." And, "But my righteous one will live by faith. And I take no pleasure in the one who shrinks back." But we do not belong to those who shrink back and are destroyed, but to those who have faith and are saved."

"So, if I keep the faith, I will make it home to be saved," Ana said.

"That is one way to interpret the scripture. God gave you free will and you are exercising it now."

"By questioning His word?"

"No, by questioning your place in a universe far larger than you ever imagined. All these weeks you have wondered and doubted and questioned, but your willingness to explore your faith among the stars is perfectly normal."

"How do you know?"

"I have a complete psychological database in addition to a religious one. By cross-referencing the two, I have reached this conclusion."

She chuckled at that.

"Can you stand one more quote?"

"Hit me," she said, smiling.

"From Matthew 24:13, 'But the one who endures to the end will be saved.' That is you, Ana."

"It is, isn't it?"

She began to rise when Xander continued speaking, "I have an anecdote if would like to hear it."

"Oh?"

"I find it pertinent to our conversations."

"Go ahead."

"It involves Dr. Velvl Greene, who was a microbiologist working for NASA in the 1970s as they began considering if there was life on Mars. During this time, he was in the process of exploring his Jewish heritage so he queried the Lubavitcher Rebbe privately if this was something he should be doing.

"The Rebbe said, 'Dr. Greene, look for life on Mars! And if you don't find it there, look somewhere else in the universe for it. Because for you to sit here and say there is no life outside of planet Earth is to put limitations on the Creator, and that is not something any of His creatures can do!'

"Can you do any less, Ana?"

"No, no I can't," she said.

Floating back to her lab, Ana considered the conversation and the presence of God, even so far out here in space. She certainly was feeling better about it all and had Xander to thank. But then, again, if God was everywhere, His presence could also be found in the machine and if that was the case, then she wasn't so alone after all. The location of Heaven seemed less weighty to her, as a result.

She floated by one of the ship's windows and paused to study the stars once more. Rather than feel lost, she was looking at endless possibilities. Ana decided she could live with so many possibilities and so many directions, now content that her soul would know which way to go.

ABOUT THE AUTHORS

Ian Randal Strock (www.IanRandalStrock.com) is the owner and publisher of Gray Rabbit Publications, LLC, and its sf imprint, Fantastic Books (www.FantasticBooks.biz). He is the author of many short stories appearing in *Nature, Analog* (from which he won two AnLab Awards), and several anthologies, and of much nonfiction, including *The Presidential Book of Lists* (Random House, 2008), *Ranking the First Ladies* (Carrel Books, 2016), and *Ranking the Vice Presidents* (Carrel Books, 2016).

Award-winning author and editor **Danielle Ackley-McPhail** has worked both sides of the publishing industry for longer than she cares to admit. In 2014 she joined forces with husband Mike McPhail and friend Greg Schauer to form her own publishing house, eSpec Books (www.especbooks.com).

Her published works include six novels, *Yesterday's Dreams, Tomorrow's Memories, Today's Promise, The Halfling's Court, The Redcaps' Queen,* and *Baba Ali and the Clockwork Djinn,* written with Day Al-Mohamed. She is also the author of the solo collections *A Legacy of Stars, Consigned to the Sea, Flash in the Can,* and *Transcendence,* the non-fiction writers' guide, *The Literary Handyman,* and is the senior editor of the *Bad-Ass Faeries* anthology series, *Gaslight & Grimm, Dragon's Lure,* and *In an Iron Cage.* Her short stories are included in numerous other anthologies and collections.

She is a member of Broad Universe, a writer's organization focusing on promoting the works of women authors in the speculative genres.

Danielle lives in New Jersey with husband and fellow writer, Mike McPhail and three extremely spoiled cats. She can be found on Facebook (Danielle Ackley-McPhail) and Twitter (DMcPhail).

Jody Lynn Nye lists her main career activity as 'spoiling cats.' When not engaged upon this worthy occupation, she writes fantasy and science fiction books and short stories.

Before breaking away from gainful employment to write full time, Jody worked as a file clerk, book-keeper at a small publishing house, freelance journalist and photographer, accounting assistant and costume maker.

For four years, she was on the technical operations staff of a local Chicago television station, WFBN (WGBO), serving the last year as Technical Operations Manager. During her time at WFBN, she was part of the engineering team that built the station, acted as Technical Director during live sports broadcasts, and worked to produce in-house spots and public service announcements.

Since 1987 she has published over 45 books and more than 150 short stories. Among the novels Jody has written are her epic fantasy series, *The Dreamland*, beginning with *Waking In Dreamland*, five contemporary humorous fantasies, *Mythology 101*, *Mythology Abroad*, *Higher Mythology* (the three collected by Meisha Merlin Publishing as *Applied Mythology*), *Advanced Mythology*, *The Magic Touch*, and three medical science fiction novels, *Taylor's Ark, Medicine Show* and *The Lady and the Tiger*. *Strong Arm Tactics*, a humorous military science fiction novel, the first of *The Wolfe Pack* series. Jody also wrote *The Dragonlover's Guide to Pern*, a non-fiction-style guide to the world of internationally best-selling author Anne McCaffrey's popular world. She also collaborated with Anne McCaffrey on four science fiction novels, *The Death of Sleep, Crisis On Doona* (*New York Times* and *USA Today* bestseller), *Treaty At Doona* and *The Ship Who Won*, and wrote a solo sequel to The Ship Who Won entitled *The Ship Errant*. Jody co-authored the *Visual Guide to Xanth* with best-selling fantasy author Piers Anthony. She has edited two anthologies, humorous stories about mothers in science fiction, fantasy, myth and legend, entitled *Don't Forget Your Spacesuit, Dear!*, and *Launch Pad*, an anthology of science fiction stories co-edited with Mike Brotherton. She wrote eight books with the late Robert Lynn Asprin, *License Invoked*, a contemporary fantasy set in New Orleans, and seven set in Asprin's *Myth Adventures* universe: *Myth-Told Tales* (anthology), *Myth Alliances*, *Myth-Taken Identity, Class Dis-Mythed, Myth-Gotten Gains, Myth Chief*, and *Myth-Fortunes*. Since Asprin's passing, she has published *Myth-Quoted, Dragons Deal* and *Dragons Run* (Ace Books), third and fourth in Asprin's *Dragons* series. Her newest series is the Lord Thomas Kinago books, beginning with *View From the Imperium* (Baen Books), a humorous military SF novel.

Her newest books are *Rhythm of the Imperium*, third in the Lord Thomas Kinago series; an e-collection of cat stories, *Cats Triumphant!* (Event Horizon), *Wishing on a Star*, part of the *Stellar Guild* series, with Angelina Adams, (Arc Manor Press) and a collection of holiday stories, *A Circle of Celebrations* (WordFire Press) , and her novella in the second in the *Clan of the Claw* series, *Tooth and Claw*.

Coming next in the pipeline is the next Myth-Adventures novel, *Myth-Fits*, scheduled for June 2016, and a young adult science fiction series co-authored with Travis S. Taylor.

Over the last twenty or so years, Jody has taught in numerous writing workshops and participated on hundreds of panels covering the subjects of writing and being published at science-fiction conventions. She has also spoken in schools and libraries around the north and northwest suburbs. In 2007 she taught fantasy writing at Columbia College Chicago. She also runs the two-day writers workshop at DragonCon.

Jody lives in the northwest suburbs of Chicago, with her husband Bill Fawcett, a writer, game designer, military historian and book packager, and a black cat, Jeremy. Check out her websites at www.jodynye.com and mythadventures.net. She is on Facebook as Jody Lynn Nye and Twitter @JodyLynnNye.

Peter Prellwitz has been writing stories, plays and skits since the fifth grade. As a child and young adult, Peter saw limited publication of one play and two series of children's puppet skits. Just enough to hook him for life.

Presently, Peter has a total of nine novels published in trade paperback and ebook, all by Double Dragon Publishing. His novel *Horizons* was selected by Mike Resnick as Best Science Fiction and awarded that publisher's 2003 Draco Award. Four of his short stories appear in the anthology *Twisted Tails*, which won the 2006 Dream Realms. Five of his novels have also been finalists in the Epic Awards over the past few years. He continues writing novels and short stories. Six more short stories have appeared in the *Defending the Future*; the *Bad-Ass Faeries*; and the *Twisted Tails* anthologies. Another is scheduled for release in 2017.

Together with more than two dozen short stories located on his site, Peter's novels help weave a tapestry of mankind's exploration and settling of the galaxy over the next two and half millennia in his ongoing Shards Universe.

A native Arizonan, Peter has also lived in Wisconsin, California, Hawaii, New York, Massachusetts, and Pennsylvania, where he now lives with his wife, Bethlynne. In addition to writing, Peter enjoys history, backpacking, and languages.

http://ShardsUniverse.net

Jeff Young is a bookseller first and a writer second – although he wouldn't mind a reversal of fortune. He is an award winning author who contributed to the anthologies: *Writers of the Future v.26, By Any Means, Best Laid Plans, Dogs of War, Man and Machine, The Best of Defending the Future, In an Iron Cage, Fantastic Futures 13, Clockwork Chaos, TV Gods, The Society for the Preservation of C.J. Henderson,* and *Gaslight and Grimm.*

Jeff's work was also published in the magazines *eSteampunk, Realms, Cemetery Moon, Trail of Indiscretion, Realms Beyond, Carbon14* and *Neuronet.* He is also an editor with Fortress Publishing for their *Drunken Comic Book Monkey* line as well as the anthology *TV Gods* and the upcoming *TV Gods - Summer Programming.* Fortress recently published a collection of his work entitled   . Jeff has helped run the Watch the Skies SF&F Reading Group of Harrisburg and Camp Hill for more than sixteen years. Finally, Jeff is also the proprietor of the online eBay and Etsy shops- Helm Haven, which produce Renaissance and Steampunk costume pieces

Patrick Thomas has had stories published in over three dozen magazines and more than fifty anthologies. He's written 30+ books including the fantasy humor series *Murphy's Lore,* urban fantasy spin offs *Fairy With A Gun, Fairy Rides The Lightning, Dead To Rites, Rites of Passage, Lore & Dysorder* and two more in the *Startenders* series. He co-writes the *Mystic Investigators* paranormal mystery series and *The Assassins' Ball,* a traditional mystery, co-authored with John L. French. His darkly humorous advice column *Dear Cthulhu* includes the collections *Cthulhu Knows Best, Have A Dark Day, Good Advice For Bad People,* and *Cthulhu Knows Best.* His latest collection is the Steampunk themed *As The Gears Turn.* A number of his books were part of the props department of the CSI television show and one was even thrown at a suspect. Fairy With A Gun was optioned by Laurence Fishburne's Cinema Gypsy Productions. *Act of Contrition*, a story featuring his Soul For Hire hitman is in development as a short film by Top Men Productions. Drop by www.patthomas.net to learn more.

James Chambers writes tales of horror, crime, fantasy, and science fiction. He is the author of *The Engines of Sacrifice*, a collection of four Lovecraftian-inspired novellas published by Dark Regions Press which *Publisher's Weekly* described in a starred-review as "…chillingly evocative…." He is also the author of the short fiction collections *Resurrection House* (Dark Regions Press) *as well as* the dark, urban fantasy novella, *Three Chords of Chaos* and *The Dead Bear Witness* and *Tears of Blood*, volume one and two in the Corpse Fauna novella series.

His short stories have been published in the anthologies *The Avenger: Roaring Heart of the Crucible, Chiral Mad 2, Clockwork Chaos, Dark Furies, The Dead Walk, Deep Cuts, The Domino Lady: Sex as a Weapon, Dragon's Lure, Fantastic Futures 13, Gaslight and Grimm, The Green Hornet Chronicles, Hardboiled Cthulhu, In An Iron Cage, Kolchak the Night Stalker: Passages of the Macabre, Shadows Over Main Street, The Spider: Extreme Prejudice, Qualia Nous, Reel Dark, Truth or Dare, TV Gods, Walrus Tales, Warfear, and the award-winning Bad-Ass Faeries and Defending the Future* series as well as the magazines *Bare Bone, Cthulhu Sex,* and *Allen K's In-human.* He has also edited and written numerous comic books including *Leonard Nimoy's Primortals,* the critically acclaimed "The Revenant" in *Shadow House,* and the original graphic novel *Kolchak, the Night Stalker: The Forgotten Lore of Edgar Allan Poe.*

His website is www.jameschambersonline.com.

Robert E Waters had been writing and publishing stories since 2003, with his first publication in *Weird Tales.* Since then, he has published over 30 stories in various print and on-line magazines and anthologies, including e-Spec's WIERD WILD WEST and the "Defending the Future" Mil SF anthology series. Robert is also a frequent contributor to Eric Flint's alternate history series, *1632/Ring of Fire,* with several stories published in the on-line *Grantville Gazette,* and most recently in Baen Book's *Ring of Fire IV* anthology. Robert's first novel, *The Wayward Eight: A Contract to Die For,* was released in 2014 under the Zmok imprint, and is a "weird wild west" adventure set in the *Wild West*

Exodus gaming universe. Robert lives in Baltimore, Maryland with his wife Beth, their son Jason, and their cat Buzz.

John L. French has worked for over thirty years as a crime scene investigator and has seen more than his share of murders, shootings and serious assaults. As a break from the realities of his job, he writes science fiction, pulp, horror, fantasy, and, of course, crime fiction.

In 1992 John began writing stories based on his training and experiences on the streets of Baltimore. His first story "Past Sins" was published in Hardboiled Magazine and was cited as one of the best Hardboiled stories of 1993. More crime fiction followed, appearing in Alfred Hitchcock's Mystery Magazine, the Fading Shadows magazines and in collections by Barnes and Noble. Association with writers like James Chambers and the late, great C.J. Henderson led him to try horror fiction and to a still growing fascination with zombies and other undead things. His first horror story "The Right Solution" appeared in Marietta Publishing's *Lin Carter's Anton Zarnak*. Other horror stories followed in anthologies such as *The Dead Walk* and *Dark Furies*, both published by Die Monster Die books. It was in *Dark Furies* that his character Bianca Jones made her literary debut in "21 Doors," a story based on an old Baltimore legend and a creepy game his daughter used to play with her friends.

John's first book was *The Devil of Harbor City*, a novel done in the old pulp style. *Past Sins* and *Here There Be Monsters* followed. John was also consulting editor for Chelsea House's *Criminal Investigation* series. His other books include *The Assassins' Ball* (written with Patrick Thomas), *Paradise Denied, Blood Is the Life, The Nightmare Strikes,* and *Monsters Among Us.* John is the editor of *To Hell in a Fast Car, Mermaids 13,* C. J. Henderson's *Challenge of the Unknown,* and (with Greg Schauer) *With Great Power ...*

You can find John on Facebook or you can email him at him at jfrenchfam@aol.com.

Christopher M. Hiles is a nurse and emergency manager specializing in Mass Casualty and Mass Fatality Incidents. He serves in the Civil Air Patrol, the United States Air Force Auxiliary, where he has held the position of Squadron Commander and Wing Health Services Officer. His work appears in *Dogs of War*. He lives in Baltimore, Maryland, with his wife and puppy.

Judi Fleming works as a training specialist and instructional designer for the federal government in her day job and thus much of her writing is of the non-exciting technical sort. She is a graduate of Seton Hill University Writing Popular Fiction Master's Program. Her stories have appeared in *No Man's Land, Best Laid Plans,* and *Dogs of War.*

Nancy Jane Moore is the author of *The Weave,* a military science fiction novel published in 2015 by Aqueduct Press, along with several other books and numerous short stories and essays.

A native Texan, she spent many years in Washington, DC, and now lives in Oakland, California. Moore has trained in martial arts since 1979 and holds a fourth-degree black belt in Aikido. She is a member of the authors' co-op Book View Café, and blogs weekly at http://bookviewcafe.com/blog/. http://nancyjanemoore.com/

Robert Greenberger is a writer and editor. He has worked for Starlog Press, where he created *Comics Scene,* the first nationally distributed magazine to focus on comic books, comic strips, and animation, DC Comics, Marvel Comics, *Weekly World News, Famous Monsters of Filmland,* ComicMix.com, and is a founding member of Crazy 8 Press. His dozens of books, short stories, and essays include *Hellboy II: The Golden Army,* for which he won the IAMTW's Scribe Award, and *The Further Adventures of Sherlock Holmes: Murder at Sorrow's Crown,* co-written with Steven Savile. He is a member of the Science Fiction Writers of America and the International Association of Media Tie-In Writers, and holds a Master of Science in Education from the University of Bridgeport and a Master of Arts in Creative Writing & Literature for Educators from Fairleigh Dickinson University.

Author and graphic artist **Mike McPhail** is member of the Military Writers Society of America; he is dedicated to helping his fellow service members (and those deserving civilians) in their efforts to become authors/editors/artist, as well as supporting related organization in their efforts to help those "who have given their all for us." www.milscifi.com

His love of science, technology, and developing an understanding of the human condition play an important role in his writing, art, and game design, all of which are built upon his training as an aeronautical engineer and dreams of becoming a NASA mission specialist, balanced by his enlistment in the service. www.mikemcphail.com

In the late 80s he was involved in game design, namely the Martial Role-Playing Game (All'Arc MRPG), a manual-based, hardcore military science fiction adventure, set in his Alliance Archives universe; sections of which are being reissued under the title of From The Archives (FT'Arc) by AGM Publications, a division of eSpec Books, LLC.

He is best known as the editor and illustrator of the award-winning Defending The Future series of military science fiction anthologies, which just celebrated its tenth anniversary with its Best Of... collection, and the continuation of the series. www.defendingthefuture.com

In 2014 he added the title of publisher, as the co-founder of eSpec Books LLC, Electronic Speculative Fiction Publishing. www.especbooks.com

KICKSTARTER ROLL CALL

Adam Selby-Martin
Alain Fournier
Alan Danziger
Anders M. Ytterdahl
Andreas Gustafsson
Andrew Hatchell
Andrew J Clark IV
Angela Carlson
Ann Stolinsky
Anonymous
Anonymous Reader
Anton Kukal
Aramanth Dawe
Arthur W. Lobdell
Ashley Knight
Ayelet Benson
Barbara and Carl Kesner
Brenda Cooper
Brendan Lonehawk
Brent Millis
Brian Bishop
Brian 'Commodore Stargazer' Whitcraft
Bryan Geddes
Candace R. Benefiel
Carol Ann Kukal
Cathy Franchett
Chad Bowden
Chand Svare Ghei
chasvag.com
Charles Anchors
Cheri Kannarr
Chris Volcheck
Colin Lloyd

Curtis & Maryrita Steinhour
Dave Hermann
Dave Lewis
David McDermott
David Mortman
Dorothy O'Hare
D-Rock
edward zagadinow
eerian sadow
Erin Penn
Evaristo Ramos, Jr.
Fan of Words
Fran Stewart
Gareth Pendleton
Gavran
Glenn Goldman
GMark Cole
Greg Resnik
Guy McLimore
Hamel Moric
Hiram G Wells
Holly Hunt
Ian Harvey
Isaac 'Will It Work' Dansicker
Ivan Donati
J.R. Murdock
Jakub Narebski
James Chambers
James Rowland
James W. Armstrong-Wood
Janine K. Spendlove
Janito Vaqueiro Ferreira Filho
Jason F. Broadley
Jason Genser

Jason Russell
Jay Zastrow
Jessica Enfante
Jessica Reid
Jiri "Picky" Cerny
John "Shadowcat" Ickes
John G. Hartness
John Green
John Idlor
John L. French
Joyce Ann Garcia from
McAllen Texas
Judy Waidlich
JW
Karen and James Henson
Karl Gallagher
Keith Hall
Keith Tracton
Keith West, Future Potentate
of the Solar System
Kelly Farmer
Ken Mencher
Kerry aka Trouble
Lady Ozma
Lark Cunningham
Lauren Hoffman
Laurie Gailunas
Laurie Hicks
Lennhoff Family
Lisa Kruse
Louise Lowenspets
Louise McCulloch
M A Pugliese
M. L. Falkenstein
M. Menzies
Marc "mad" Winkelmann
Margaret St. John
Mark Knapp Jr
Mark Lukens

Martin Bernstein
Mary Spila
Mat Masding-Grouse
Matt P
Matthew Hieb
Max Kaehn
mdtommyd
Michael Carson
Michael D Blanchard
Michael Fedrowitz
Michael Skolnik
Mike Maurer
Nathan Duby
Nathan Turner
Neil A Ottenstein
Nellie B.
Nicole McPherson
Niki Coppola
Pat Hayes
Patrick Thomas
Paul Ryan
Paul van Oven
Pepita Hogg-Sonnenberg
Peter Thew
Peter Young
R.T. Bryson
Ralph M. Seibel
Raymond Finch
Revek
RK Bookman
Rob Karp
Robby Thrasher
Robert E Waters
Roisin mcCormac
Ross Hathaway
Roy Romasanta
S Ruskin
sam murphy
Samuel Lubell

Scott A Johnson
Scott Elson
Scott Mayanrd
Scott Schaper
Sean McGarry
Sebastian H.
ShadowCub
Shervyn
Sheryl R. Hayes
Silence in the Library
    Publishing
Simo Muinonen
Simon Clark
Soldier Systems Daily
Stephanie Lucas
Stephen A, Fender
Stephen Ballentine
Stephen Cheng
Suragai
Susan Carlson
Susan R Grossman

Svend Andersen
SwordFire
Tamara Michelle Slaten
thatraja
The loyal minion, Linda
Thomas M. Karwacki Jr.
Thomas Werner
Tina England
Tina Noe Good
Tom Berrisford
Tomas Burgos-Caez
Tony Finan
Tory Shade
Towelman
V. Hartman DiSanto
Vickie B
Wallace MacBix
Wes Rist
William Hughes
William Wiebking